George Allender

Imbroglio

a drama

George Allender

Imbroglio
a drama

ISBN/EAN: 9783337374686

Printed in Europe, USA, Canada, Australia, Japan

Cover: Foto ©Andreas Hilbeck / pixelio.de

More available books at **www.hansebooks.com**

IMBROGLIO

A DRAMA

BY

GEORGE ALLENDER

SAN FRANCISCO
SAMUEL CARSON & CO., PUBLISHERS
120 SUTTER STREET
1885

DRAMATIS PERSONÆ.

———   .

EDMUND MALONE.

HAROLD,
RICHARD, } Sons of Malone.

HENCHMAN.

GLASCO.

MAURICE BOURNE.

A WHITE FORM.

A BLACK FORM.

A MAN, and A WOMAN.

CATHERINE, wife of Malone.

CHARLOTTE,
HELEN, } Daughters of Malone.

HORTENS TECHNOR.

SCENE OF PLAY: CALIFORNIA.

TO THEATRICAL MANAGERS.

It is not imagined that any manager would care to risk his reputation by the production of this play. Nor that any one would appropriate it to his own use without the author's consent. But if there be any one who has an inclination in these directions, he may be reminded that the copyright laws of the United States protect DRAMATIC as well as other literary productions, and that the author will insist on his rights.

THE AUTHOR.

IMBROGLIO.

———o———

ACT I.

SCENE.—MALONE'S *country house; a room looking out upon a park.*

Present, CATHERINE MALONE.

O wretched woman I, in this great change!
Poor was I then, but not this poverty.
Then was I not a wife, yet husbandless.
What is my fault—what dreadful crime is mine—
That he should hate me so, nor tell me why?

Enter MALONE *(*CATHERINE *approaches him and is repelled).*

O Edmund, do not turn me from you thus.
If business cares, or any fault of mine,
Have made you mingle with your silence sighs,
And look at me in this mysterious way,
Unbosom it to her you used to love.

(He again repels her, sighing.)

Ah me! I am your wife in name alone.

(Exit CATHERINE.*)*

MALONE.

And would to Heaven you were not even that.

Her very love grows hateful to my sense.
She is the murderer of my advancement,
The thief who robs me of the vantage
Of my wealth, steals my best occasions,
Lays waste my fairest chances, stands me still;
Till in my millions I am yet so poor
There is no cheerful beggar but I envy.

Enter HENCHMAN.

HENCHMAN.

I think I see your heart upon your face.

MALONE.

I would I had your eyes to see the heart.

HENCHMAN.

Eyes which see hearts are much preferred to hearts
Which can be seen by eyes, as the world wags.
But in the name of pills and physic,
What means this melancholy eyeing?

MALONE.

Doctor, nothing is merry in my mood.

HENCHMAN.

Tut, man! has your liver or your broker
Played you false?   I would think you sure in love.

MALONE.

Would that I knew the sources of our loves.

HENCHMAN.

They lie in dungeons where philosophers
And fools alike are without eyes and ears.

Betwixt two hearts in love there plays a force
So gently fine that only love can note it.

MALONE.

That is the hot love of our poet days;
But for our winter wear must there not be
A certain similarity in lovers' ways?

HENCHMAN.

I made a poem on that subject once.

MALONE.

Can you recall it?

HENCHMAN (*trying to recollect*).

       Humph!—we will grow old—
It has been an age since my brain labored
In love's service—"Similitude of thoughts"—
"Similitude of thoughts is love's main-sail,
Of ways and tastes and likes, its peaceful stream,
Of nature's gifts, its everchanging verdure,
And hearts thus joined live in unending spring."—
The rhyme is off—"live an unending dream."
"But when a man, by nature mighty made,
Is to a woman of inferior graces joined"—

                        (Pauses.)

MALONE.

I think I could almost fill out the lines.

HENCHMAN.

"Though for a time he make a toy of her,
She, in the end, will bring him foul disgust."
The rhythm is most monstrously awry.

MALONE.

The sense can well forego the rhyme's presence.
I know a friend who has a wife like that.
What figure think you beauty cuts in love?

HENCHMAN.

No gentleman with fine æsthetic tastes
Can ever love a merely ugly woman.

MALONE.

What if she be ignorant and ugly, too?

HENCHMAN.

Heaven defend! why, such a wretch should have
A husband ignorant and ugly, too.

MALONE.

If to those virtues you add jealousy?

HENCHMAN.

You were two holes in hell at last counting!
I would sooner summer with the devil
Than winter with a jealous woman.
But what occasion has this questioning?

MALONE.

Doctor, your merry mind but little knows
That in the height of my apparent fortune
I live in the very dregs of misery.

HENCHMAN (*with apparent feeling*).

I beg your pardon for my levity.
I thought that rich and happy were one word;
For I have tramped so long in poverty
I thought that it alone was misery.

MALONE.

This hoard of wealth you see is as the sun
That brings my hidden misery to light,
Uncloaks the ghastly form of my despair,
Strips off the gaudy furbelows from one
Who entertained the unappreciative eye
Of poverty, showing me to myself.
You see these arbors, variegated flowers,
These waving fields and picture landscapes:—
They are but deserts of a common hue.
Music—it is a humdrum monotone;
The fairest food sickens my appetite,
And all my feelings, thoughts, desires have slunk
So low into my shrouded spirit's depths
That, come these pleasures through whatever sense,
They all are darkened by my mind's despair.

HENCHMAN.

For this depression there must be grave cause.

MALONE.

Yes, cause and cause enough—a spectre cause!
Uncalled it comes fawning o'er my shoulder,
Stares in my face, follows me in my walk,
Crawls to my bed, haunts me in my company,
Till I am dead with chafing and chagrin.

HENCHMAN.

Would that I had the skill to serve you here.

MALONE.

I have known you better than I have known
You long; but if these features, bearing the stamp

Of honesty, be not a mockery
Of nature, a man may place his troubles
In your keeping.

HENCHMAN.

Poor am I in the world,
But honest in my heart.

MALONE.

I believe you,
And, if you will, shall make my cause your own.
This wife of mine, if wife that may be named
Which is a little something more than beast—
Be not surprised, I know whereof I speak—
This wifely incubus, which, shaming nature,
Has, like a dismal fever, grown upon me;
This wife-name of wifely attributes devoid—
As love, refined desire, respect, esteem,
In her not found, in me all uninspired,
And in their stead disgust, foul as a toad,
Shame and loathing, rendering all approach
Unbearable, hatred without reprieve—
This thing has come to be a ghastly shade,
Haunting and dogging me unceasingly;
One which in my poverty I had not,
Not knowing that I had it, but, being rich,
The skeleton is always in my eyes.
Of all the beggary I ever heard,
The meanest pauper in this world is he
Who has a wife of whom he is ashamed.
See, there she comes!   Oh, forty times a day
Would scarce enumerate her cursed calls!

(*Exit* MALONE, *hurriedly.*)

HENCHMAN.

How timidly she comes, as though her tread
Were o'er a grave; perhaps it is her own.—
A spectre legacy of his dead life!
A ghastly skeleton he aptly called it.
Well, you are wedded to your skeleton,
And in the beaten ways of married life
You must eat with it, must let it put
Its hideous, tasteless lips upon your own,
Must to your bosom hug its loathesome form,
Must let it occupy your hated bed,
And clank and rattle its disgusting bones
Against your tender flesh; or else, or else—
Ho! Henchman, is not here a goodly chance
To make a hard bed easy for your life?

Enter CATHERINE, *to the door.*

CATHERINE.

Is that you, Doctor Henchman?

HENCHMAN.

Madam, yes;
And is there ought that he can do for you?

CATHERINE.

Is not my husband here?

HENCHMAN.

A moment since
Your husband left. (*Aside.*) Quack, lover, lawyer,
    priest—
And first the last. Ah, lady, what grief is this

That seems so trying to your tender heart?
Nay, do not sigh so deep; there is a balm
In Gilead for every bruised breast,
And dear confession for the soul is best.
(*Aside*) The devil take me! that ice is venturesome.

CATHERINE.

Oh, Doctor, you are learned in all the things
That great men know—

HENCHMAN (*aside*).

A little more than fool.

CATHERINE.

Has not my husband some most dire disease?

HENCHMAN (*with importance*).

Some little time ago your husband passed
An era of most consequental illness;
But that he is entirely recovered
I am convinced, at least I wholly think so.

CATHERINE.

You think so, Doctor? but, truly tell me,
Is not that ailment lingering in him still?

HENCHMAN.

Perhaps, madam, in that relationship,
So intimate, so tender, and so dear,
That dwells between a husband and his wife,
You have seen things which I, in chance observe
Have let pass by unnoticed.   Nay, madam,
If you would have my aid, give confidence.

CATHERINE.

As you are his doctor I will tell you,

Hoping that you may therefrom give him aid.
Once he was gentle and so kind, but now
He is so harsh, alas, so cruel harsh!
And unto me, who never did him wrong.

HENCHMAN.

Such symptoms are, indeed, most dangerous;
But I will watch him in his every mood,
And do what lies within my scope to help him.

CATHERINE.

Then on you rest the blessings of a wife,
Who loves her husband better than her life (*going*).

Enter MAURICE BOURNE.

Ah, Maurice! I thought you had forsaken us.

BOURNE.

Forsaken you? why, bless my life! what made you think so? I have been so monstrous busy in the mines of late I have not had the time to come, but, being at the bay—ah, doctor!

HENCHMAN.

How are you, sir?

BOURNE.

In a fair way for one who loves the world too much. As I say, being at the bay, I thought I would come down and spend a day or two in your new home. Are the children home from college yet?

CATHERINE.

I knew it was the children you had come to see. They will be home to-day.

BOURNE.

So Harold wrote me.   How's Malone?   I should
like to see him.

CATHERINE.

We will go and find him, Maurice.

BOURNE.

Kate, it seems to me you are not looking well.

CATHERINE.

Never better, never better in my life.

(*Exeunt* CATHERINE *and* BOURNE.)

HENCHMAN.

Something is here:—I recollect Malone
Once told me that this fellow loved his wife
Before he married her.   A shadow's shadow's
Food enough to fat an army of suspicions.

Re-enter MALONE.

MALONE (*speaking of* BOURNE).

I know that voice that always laughs at me,
And with more quib than wit forever rails.

HENCHMAN.

I warrant it; his ways are mean in that.
But then you know, Malone, there are some men
Who, being the cause of others' misery,
Can well afford to be hilarious,
And with a kind of caustic raillery
Slabber their victims o'er.   Oh, there are men,
And men in plenty, in this world like that.

MALONE.

I would the devil had all men like him.

HENCHMAN.

I am warm in the merit of your cause;
For I have watched the current married world
To find the reason of its great disorder;
And I have seen a host of wedded men,
On whom kind nature heaped her richest stores,
Who by a fault of their unthinking youth
Have married women much beneath their grade.
Then when the era of awakening came—

MALONE.

Oh, when the era of awakening comes!

HENCHMAN.

And they behold their joindure thus awry,
Their lives fall in a rot, these mighty ships
Stripped sailless in mid ocean, where they float
To chafe the waves and turn to water-logs.

MALONE.

Oh, how my life fits in the die of your
Description! Your wisdom, sir, is great.

HENCHMAN.

Mere nothing, man! These are but facts which fools
In the mad house, twenty to the score can see;
But the value of all facts lies in their
Inference.   To be unhappy married
Is one thing, but to know the cause thereof,
And to provide a remedy, puzzles
Philosophers and stands our legislators.

MALONE.

In faith, I think, to do so must be so.

2

HENCHMAN.

Unpleasant truths most oft to error lead;
Distasteful facts are cunning to deceive;
Mistaken marriage is the broad highway
To desecrated homes and blasted lives.
Yet wise men in their foolish wisdom hold
That happiness is nurtured, vice made less,
By keeping these distorted things in state;
While I, poor fool! of foolish wisdom void,
Would cure the evil in its primal cause—
Unloose the band of each mismated pair,
And set the tortured birds at liberty.

MALONE.

Sir, I have heard you speak of poverty;
And now I shame myself, that, being rich,
In my lament I have not thought of yours.
Henceforth my purse is open as my heart.

HENCHMAN (*feigning*).

I have a sudden weakness overcomes me.
Dear sir, I have no words to give you thanks.

MALONE.

Nor need have none; kind actions best are thanks.

HENCHMAN.

Oh, that I had the might to dress my thanks in acts.

MALONE.

And so you have if you will but devise
A plan to rid me of this incubus.

HENCHMAN.

This is sudden like—I will think on it.

MALONE.

There is no reason for concealment here;
Give me your unpremeditated thoughts.

HENCHMAN.

It were best the matter lay in the mind
A night; I cannot think so suddenly.

MALONE (*giving him his pocket book*).

Receive this in the name of friendship, sir;
A pittance for kindness, not for service.

HENCHMAN.

Ah, Malone, I, who have been kicked and cuffed
By this cold, heartless world, appreciate
The magnanimity of such a friend.

MALONE.

To me the sum is nothing. Lift this load
And I will give you such a sum as will,
In its mere interest, keep you for your life
In all the luxury your mind can wish.

HENCHMAN.

You will do that? You will take this hungry wolf
And strangle him? You will brace these old legs
While going down the declivity of time?
You will do this?—ah, then I bear my heart;
I tell you what my eyes have seen; which, but
For this and for your friendly misery,
Had, for a woman's sake, been sealed forever.
How this complex emotion stirs my soul!
(*Laughs aside as if weeping.*)

MALONE (*aside*).

I think the offer takes his conscience in.

HENCHMAN.

'There need be no invention for your cause,
Where now too much reality exists;
But, for the modesty of womanhood,
Will not your wife consent to a divorce?

MALONE.

As masters free their slaves!   I am her serf,
So mean that she will neither give nor sell
Me liberty, slicking her tyranny
With talk of the divinity of marriage,
And pat old proverbs, soaked in ignorance,
Of children's rights, society's great claim,
Of wives and husbands in the world to come,
And all the priestly clap-trap she has learned.

HENCHMAN.

And, if she had good cause, do you not think
She would herself proceed for a divorce?

MALONE.

Not though I charged her nose with the foul stench
Of all debauchery, and run the gamut
Of every legal cause before her eyes.

HENCHMAN (*aside*).

How vain these husbands are!   The shameless thing!
Then you yourself must take the plaintiff's part.

MALONE.

In Heaven's name, upon what ground may I?

HENCHMAN.

If you had seen what I have seen, and what,
I take it, any man with eyes might see,
You would not ask, *upon what ground may I.*
Did you not tell me that this fellow Bourne—

MALONE.

Do you hear, Henchman, I have come to hate
That much loved man, my partner though he be
With hatred such as one dares scarcely own.

HENCHMAN.

I doubt not you have ample cause for hate.

MALONE.

Why, so I have: Malone is but the shade,
Bourne the mighty sun of all we do.

HENCHMAN.

Poh, man! that is a ground for children's fights.
You have a graver cause to hate this man.

MALONE.

Do you think so?

HENCHMAN.

As certainly as sin.
Did you not tell me once that Maurice loved
Your wife before you married her? *(Aside.)* Well,
    laugh!

MALONE.

Why, now, you make me laugh. Yes, so he did,
But what has that to do with my dislike?
You think me jealous?—now you make me laugh.

HENCHMAN.

Tum! tum! there is much music that is never heard.

MALONE.

Why, that was five and twenty years ago.

HENCHMAN.

A good long period for secret work.—
You won your wife spite of Maurice's wooing?

MALONE.

And would to Heaven he had drawn the prize.
I would most willingly convey it to him
By deed of gift.

HENCHMAN.

Perhaps there is no need.
That eldest son *of yours* has not your eyes.

MALONE *(with interest)*.

So?—why, now, I never noticed that.

HENCHMAN.

Your youngest daughter Helen's monstrous fair,
With golden locks, for parents dark as hers.

MALONE.

I have observed and often thought of that.

HENCHMAN.

It is a marvelous phenomenon,
A great perturbation in old nature,
When children white are of black parents born

MALONE.

Something is most mysterious in this.

HENCHMAN.

Climate, sir, California climate.

MALONE.

Indeed, doctor, this is a serious joke.

HENCHMAN.

I used it to that purpose once.

.   MALONE.

You did?

HENCHMAN.

Your wife and this *fair* Bourne, Helen and I—
You being away were once conversing.
"Madam," said I, "how wondrous *fair* she is,"
Meaning Helen.

MALONE.

You said that, what said she?

HENCHMAN.

Not a word.

MALONE.

Not a word?—Dumfounded guilt!

HENCHMAN.

But you had been amazed, if not amused,
To see how crimsoned up her face became.

MALONE.

You say she blushed?

HENCHMAN.

A sure indicative
Of certain guilt—*(aside)* or beauteous modesty.

MALONE *(aside)*.

There's more than plotting here.— When took this
    place ?

HENCHMAN.

You mean the blush ?

MALONE.

         Heaven and earth, how keen
That dagger is !

HENCHMAN.

      This does not hurt you, sir ?

MALONE.

You run me through and ask me, *Does it hurt ?*—
No difference.   Have you seen more than this ?

HENCHMAN.

Oh, somewhat, with the eye of inference.

MALONE.

Your thoughts are too much muffled, sir; speak
    plain.

HENCHMAN.

Did you not say that, since your marriage, Bourne
Has followed you about from place to place
For all these years ?

MALONE.

         I said that he and I
Had worked and gone together through these years.

HENCHMAN.

Drown words; it is the substance that I seek.

MALONE.

Think you that Maurice had a motive there ?

HENCHMAN.

Motive? oh, no, no motive; motive! no.
Men do not act from motive in this world.
Disinterested friendship moves this world.

MALONE (*aside*).

There's an apparent venom in that speech.—
And think you these facts are inferential?

HENCHMAN.

Inferential? oh, no; nothing, it seems,
To you is inferential; but some one
Grossly suspicious might draw conclusion—

MALONE.

What conclusion, Henchman, what conclusion?

HENCHMAN.

That Maurice is a wondrous, curious man.

MALONE.

How curious? That hollow laugh has meaning.

HENCHMAN.

Meaningless as gnats,—monstrous credulity!
Yet, in the trodden way of common sense,
It is a little strange, or ludicrous,
That Bourne should have followed you, or, rather,
Shall I say your—ah! no difference—lived,
Did you not say, in the same house, and slept
In the same—ah! pardon me; I mean ate—
Devilish brotherly!— at the same table?

MALONE.

Henchman, you have seen that you dare not tell.

HENCHMAN.

I have seen that—

MALONE.

You have seen what, Henchman?

HENCHMAN.

How monstrous color-blind a husband is
To that another man may see—with his nose.

MALONE.

Ha! this interests me not.   I care not
For this woman, though one and all the men—

HENCHMAN.

Nor for your children either, I suppose.

MALONE.

Dare you cast suspicion on my children?

HENCHMAN.

I did not *do* it.

MALONE (*aside*).

Fool to be thus touched!—
And think you this fellow still loves my wife?

HENCHMAN.

Loves, man?—think! O, villainous presumption
That fish should lose their taste for water ways!

MALONE.

O, doctor, these dark insinuations—

HENCHMAN.

Insinuations?

MALONE.

And deep conclusions
Are the very logic of unkindness,
Do you imagine; lies it in fancy—

HENCHMAN.

My dear sir, fancy is reason's ruin.
When I became a doctor I buried
My imagination with my first patient—
Till resurrection, *requiescant in pace.*
I simply put together this and that,—
Eyes, hair, complexion, love of long standing,
Opportunity, and inclination,
The general slothfulness of husbands;
And from this matrix draw conclusion forth
That all these years you have been made a dupe.

MALONE.

Heaven and earth, how rises now the nightmare
Of the hideous past in phases multiform
To show me to mine own stupidity!

HENCHMAN (*aside*).

'Tis very well; the argument sounds *fair.*

MALONE.

Henchman, perhaps in honesty, perhaps
In perfidy, perhaps in wicked league
With these, my enemies, you put me on the rack.

HENCHMAN.

But act this part, and you'll be rid of her.

MALONE.

Act, man! your logic has all act dismayed;

Henceforth I am in substance simply this:
I care not for her, but to be the dupe
Of their foul cunning, and have suspicion
On my children cast; to be the point for wits
To shoot their venom at, the theme for jokes,—
I will at once advise with my attorney,
And bring this beastly marriage to an end.

HENCHMAN.

Softly now! be not in too much haste.

MALONE.

Time treads a sluggard pace till I have put
This woman where her acts condemn her.

HENCHMAN.

Then if you will be gone thus hastily,
When you return, fetch with you your attorney,
That he may see his cause upon the ground,
And I will show to you, or him, or any man,
What neither you, nor he, nor any man should see.

(*Exit* MALONE.)

Now for the very solace of his mind
He wants a reason for his villainy.
Shadows will do, but I will give him more;
For in this small, round compass of a brain
There lives a being that possesses might
To make a white-robed angel black as night.

(*Exit* HENCHMAN.)

Re-enter MALONE, *with his hat and overcoat.*

MALONE.

et, if I but had the eyes of love

To see these facts, what mountains would they be.
His eyes, hair his, complexion his—nonsense!
Still an array of most damnable facts—
What made me laugh at first now makes me think,
And with annoyance doubles up my hate.

Enter CATHERINE.

Why, now, I had not thought you cared so much
For my poor company in these late days.

CATHERINE.

Oh, Edmund! I have only come to say
Our children will be home to-day, and beg you
Save me in their presence from harsh treatment.

Enter HAROLD *to the door.*

MALONE.

Well, have you done.

CATHERINE.

Oh, will you not tell me—

MALONE.

Still here? Oh, you can cry, and cry, and cry.

HAROLD (*aside*).

What is't I hear?

CATHERINE.

Oh, just one little word,
And have I wronged you—

MALONE.

Have you not wronged me?

CATHERINE.

If so none knows but Heaven—

MALONE.

Nor need know.
And there are things which Heaven best know not.

CATHERINE.

If ever I have wronged you, tell me of my fault,
And I will go upon these knees and beg
Of you forgiveness, the humblest penitent
In all this world of sinners; (*kneels*) speak, Ed-
    mund.

MALONE.

That one should have the face of honesty!—
No? you will not go? Then I will leave you.
                                        (*Going.*)

CATHERINE.

Please, Edmund, tell me, for our children's sake.
        (*Exit* MALONE, *followed by* CATHERINE.)

HAROLD.

What! what! now what is this? Did I see right?
My father turned a brute—a husband beast!
Nor was he given to drinking. His mind
Must be deranged to speak so to his wife.
See where she kneels, still clinging to him,
And still beseeching him to tell her why.
Unseen I will observe their further acts,
That I may catch the clue to this offense.
                                (*Secretes himself.*)

    Enter RICHARD.

Richard! Richard!

RICHARD.

What's the matter, Harold?
You are too much given to this way of late.

HAROLD.

See where our parents come, O Richard, see!
Our mother all in tears begging our father—

RICHARD.

Something is like offense in that; listen!
(They secrete themselves.)
Re-enter MALONE *followed by* CATHERINE.

CATHERINE.

Edmund, hear me.

MALONE.

No more, no more, I say:
I will have nothing more to do with you.

HAROLD *(to* RICHARD).

Do you mark that! Now Heaven see those tears!

CATHERINE.

But why, oh why, will you not tell me why?

MALONE.

Why! why! and so let *why* your answer be
Until you ask yourself.

HAROLD.

He is turned iron.

CATHERINE.

Heaven well knows you hate me without cause.

MALONE.

Heaven well knows—O Kate! Kate! Oh, shame,
    shame!

CATHERINE.

You have gone mad. This is the curse of riches.

MALONE.

Riches, indeed! Indeed, riches! Away!
Out on this handy platitude of thieves! (*Takes
    hold of her.*)
Can you look me in the face? O Kate, shame!
                 (*Exit hurriedly.*)

CATHERINE.

Father in Heaven, open thou my heart
To any wrong I ever did my husband.
Oh, I thus harshly used could die, but that
I live to once more see my darling ones.
To me, O God, preserve my children's love;
Oh, let them not forsake me in my woe!
               (*Exit* CATHERINE.)

HAROLD *and* RICHARD *come forward.*

RICHARD.

You have eyes and ears; have you not a tongue?

HAROLD.

I would I had not either eyes or ears.

RICHARD.

Why, then, most like, you would not have a tongue.
Come, come; we have seen what children should
    not see.

HAROLD.

We did not see it; these things but seem to be.
The world does not exist but in our minds.
We are not here, but only think we are.

RICHARD.

Fling such philosophy to blind puppies!
This self-delusion is the beggar's trade.
We have seen and seen, and now where lies the
    wrong?

HAROLD.

Noted you how he sighed, as he would break
His heart, when he exclaimed, *O Kate! Oh shame.'*

RICHARD.

I tell you, Harold, I see these matters
With the plain eyes of common sense.   I say
Our mother is imposed on by these acts.

HAROLD.

O God, that we should come to find it so!

RICHARD.

Come, Harold, such things are not uncommon.

HAROLD.

Indeed, I think they must be very common.

RICHARD.

Well, we must find a way to heal this wrong.
What can be done by children we must do.
You are my elder, and have a gentler way;
Besides, our father loves you with a warmer,
But I do not say a better, love —
As nature ofttimes will demear herself.

3

Therefore to cure this matter rests with you;
I will enforce you as lies in my power.
Come, now, Harold; it may not be so bad.

HAROLD.

O Richard, I think I see much more in this
Than you are willing that your mind should see.
I hear our sisters; not a word to them.

(*They stand apart.*)

Enter CHARLOTTE *and* HELEN.

CHARLOTTE.

What means this speaking silence?   O Harold,
Is mother sick?

HELEN.

Some one is sick, I know.
Richard, what is it?   What is it, Richard?

HAROLD.

Are you not glad that you are home?
Is it not beautiful?   How changed
From the barren hills we used to see!

CHARLOTTE.

No, no, Harold; what has happened?
Tell me, Harold, what has happened.

RICHARD (*to* HELEN).

There, there, you little imp—if you must know,
Harold and I have had a little tilt.

HAROLD.

Yes, yes; your hand, Richard, your hand!

CHARLOTTE.

Now this is not the case; for I well know

That these unnatural ways and words are
But assumed, and have a meaning of their own.
If you love me, tell me why you act so.

CENTER_HAROLD.

Take them away, Richard; it is no use—
Nature thus injured cannot act a part.
Go find your mother.

CHARLOTTE *and* HELEN.

Mother!

HAROLD.

No, no; go.

In time I will relate it all to you.

(*Exeunt* CHARLOTTE *and* HELEN, *excitedly,*
followed by RICHARD.)

Yet seemed she innocent of all offense—
Heaven and earth how gross his manner was!
And after all this age of happy life
To treat her thus? And yet there seemed a kind
Of madness in his acts, and, as it were,
Offended lunacy, thrust into madness
By some offensive cause; there must be cause.

Enter BOURNE.

BOURNE.

Hello! home from college?

HAROLD.

Yes, I am here.

BOURNE.

Here, Harold! why this is not your manner.

HAROLD.

What is it? The cause, Maurice, the reason?
I know that you will tell me what it is.

BOURNE.

Cause? reason? cause for what, in Heaven's name?
What have you seen to make you act this way?

HAROLD.

Seen, Maurice, seen! now what have I not seen?
My father, Maurice, your friend, my father?

BOURNE.

Well, what of him, Harold? Is he not well?

HAROLD.

Lately have you seen nothing strange in him?
Has he forgot his friends? Speaks he not
To them crabbedly? Walks he not head-bowed,
Brow-clouded, muttering? Does he attend
Aswas his wont to business? Or has he—

BOURNE.

Pardon me, Harold, concerning these things
I am a stranger.   If with your father
You have had some trouble, go and mend it.
                              (*Exit* ₍BOURNE.)

HAROLD.

Then his complaint is special to his wife.
          Enter HENCHMAN.

HENCHMAN.

How's my young Cartesian? Ah, Harold! I am
glad to see you back, for I have much to tell you.

HAROLD.

Yes, yes; has he been sick long?

HENCHMAN.

I hear you took high honors at the University—

HAROLD.

What is his affliction, Doctor?

HENCHMAN.

And dare say you are now prepared to revolu-
tionize the world, particularly 'inmatters ethical
(*laughs*), that being a prime theme with young col-
legians.   How I remember—

HAROLD.

Please you, sir, what ailment has my father?

HENCHMAN.

Your father? ailment?   Have you not seen him?

HAROLD.

I have *seen* him, yet I have not seen *him*.

HENCHMAN.

How strange you act!   Have you but just arrived?

HAROLD.

I think I came a thousand years ago,
If time be measured by events, not clocks.
Is not my father mentally deranged?

HENCHMAN.

Have you seen ought indicative of that?

HAROLD.

I have seen, I have seen, and I have heard—
But to be direct, sir, I saw in him
Somewhat of harshness toward my mother,
And I had not observed the thing before.

HENCHMAN.

Indeed! did he accuse her of any wrong?

HAROLD.

None that I could catch; he came upon her
As a fearful hurricane sweeps down upon
An unoffending house of God.

HENCHMAN.
                          Harold,
I think your father a very honest man.

HAROLD.

Why, so did I.

HENCHMAN.
                    A conscientious man,
And that he would do no one an injustice.

HAROLD.

As such I always have esteemed my father.

HENCHMAN.

One slow to anger, of a gentle heart,
Having forgiveness strong implanted in him.

HAROLD.

Yet why acts he toward my mother thus?

HENCHMAN (*half aside*).

Perhaps he has some cause.

HAROLD.

What said you, sir?

HENCHMAN.

Nothing.

HAROLD.

Yes, but you did though, about cause.

HENCHMAN.

Oh! that surely he could not have a cause.

HAROLD.

Think you that he is causeless utterly?—
Mere malice, deliberate cruelty?

HENCHMAN.

It is not meet that I should speak of this.
Keep quiet, Harold, and closely observe.
He who sees nothing, sometimes sees the most;
Hear nothing, the better to hear it all;
Keep your ears primed and keep your tongue
    silent.
Withal, trust Henchman as your steadfast friend.

(*Exit* HENCHMAN.)

HAROLD.

Now, if I find him so, which I hope not,
If torture be his game, which I hope not—

Enter CATHERINE.

CATHERINE.

My boy, my boy, you have come home at last!
No mother ever longed to see her son
As I have longed to see you, Harold.

HAROLD.

Yes, I have come.

CATHERINE.

Oh, how the weary sun
Has dragged along, making the minutes hours,
And every hour a day, and every day a year
Till you should come.

HAROLD.

Well, mother, I am here.

CATHERINE.

Why, Harold, how strange your voice! and your
dear face
Is by deep furrows and high ridges marred.

HAROLD.

Yes; I had a sudden sickness lately.

CATHERINE.

And did not let me know it?

HAROLD.

Well, mother,
What's the news?   Have you written everything
Which has importantly occurred since I,
Some nine months past, left home?   How is father?

CATHERINE.

Well, Harold, I hope.

HAROLD.

Nay, but how is father?

CATHERINE.

Why, Harold, I do not catch the meaning
Of your strange manner.

HAROLD.

Now undeceive me,
Mother;—who than I should know this trouble.

CATHERINE.

Of what trouble do you speak?

HAROLD.

What trouble?
No more! no more! I say I will have nothing more
To do with you! Ha! can you look me in the face?
O Kate, Kate! O, shame, shame! What trouble
God!
Such as o'erthrows the sovereign majesty
Of home, topples the universe of man
And wife, flings children to the wolfish world,
And to a cinder burns up holy love.

CATHERINE.

O Harold, my heart is broke!

HAROLD.

There, mother,
I overheard him. Now, what cause has he
To thus belabor and demean his wife?

CATHERINE.

If Heaven knows, it is a secret here.

HAROLD.

What! will he assign no reason, mother?

CATHERINE.

What you have seen and heard is all I know;
Beyond this step can no appeal extend him.

HAROLD.

When came and how grew on this disposition?

CATHERINE.

A little after you had gone from home
A kind of coolness overcame your father;
He seldom spoke to me; answered me yes
And no, and grew impatient if I spoke
Too frequently to him.   Then he would sit
As in a reverie, his mind away
On distant objects, from which he waked
To glance askance at me and mutter curses.

HAROLD.

You say he would do that?

CATHERINE.

In company
My presence seemed to give him great offense;
Seeing which, I often on some trifle
Excused myself; when, pleased, he went alone;
Next, for long days he would remain away,
At which, if I but hinted at the cause,
He shortly snapped me up; and then, at length,
His manner changed—he would sigh like a moan,
Then fiercely glare at me and shame me so
As I had done some crime too bad for words.

HAROLD.

And can you not conjecture at the cause?

CATHERINE.

Oh, I have thought and thought, till dazed my
  mind

Would sink into bewilderment.   Sometimes
I think he has become deranged in mind;
Again, suspicion seizes me that since his wealth
He has outgrown me, Harold, and that now
His great ambition seeks to travel ways
Where Heaven never meant that I should follow.—
That now he looks upon me as the relic,
Much detested, of his departed state;
And that he wants a fairer face than mine.

HAROLD.

Of such depravity, so monstrous grown,
Think you the human heart is capable?

CATHERINE.

No, Harold; those names you must not call it.
But will you try some soft and gentle means
To win your father back?

HAROLD.

               If such fair means
Will the good end accomplish, mother,
None of a grosser kind shall I employ.

CATHERINE.

Well, Harold, if the most gentle pleading
Of his wife and son can make no movement
In your father's passing strange estrangement,
It is no use to try the other way.
And if we fail—

HAROLD.

       But, mother, we'll not fail.

CATHERINE.

Oh, Harold, you will not forsake me, then !

HAROLD.

Unless this little dot of earth forsakes
The mighty sun, you who are more to me
Than sun to earth, can never be forsaken.
'Twould be as though I should forsake my heart,
Forget to breathe, or put my own eyes out.

CATHERINE.

And if he will remain unmoved by us
Then I can die.   When I have passed that sphere
Where I am worthy to be called his wife;
When in his eyes I raise but foul disgust,
When sight of me produces shame in him;
When I become a stop to his ambition,—
Oh, then I want to die, I want to die !

(*Exit* CATHERINE.)

HAROLD.

Raises disgust !—shames him !—unworthy !—she?
A stop to his ambition !—my mother ?
And withal his wife, who through so many years
Of poverty and hardship followed him
His willing slave !—now when the years begin
To fall upon her—is it conceivable ?—
To be cast into the street, like a shoe
In its owner's service now past service,—
She, the mother of his children, his wife,
In sickness who watch, for him denied herself—
Oh, if I find it so, and he relent not,
Farewell all gentle ways; wipe from my heart
All love I bear him, if he prove callous !

Now may eternal justice be my guide,
And may the blackest fiends of darkness seize
My blacker soul if I defend her not!

(Exit HAROLD.)

ACT II.

SCENE.—MALONE'S *country house; a room.*

Enter HAROLD *and* CHARLOTTE.

CHARLOTTE.

Oh, act to nature foreign! Poor mother!—
I scarcely can conceive how it could be.

HAROLD.

No more could I, had I not seen the sight.

CHARLOTTE.

Oh, I am glad I did not witness it.
Such awful discord—

HAROLD.

Discord? why, Charlotte,
It was the clash of nature in rebellion.
If all at once my body had been hurled
Into a well of fierce up-pointed swords,
I could not more have suffered than I did.

CHARLOTTE.

And all your pain is imaged on my heart.
In this distressful state what shall we do?

HAROLD.

First, we must find the cause of father's acts.

If they be motiveless, that argues madness.
And so they may be; for these adventures
Into which he has been thrust so quickly,
The incident anxiety, and strain,
The whirl and dizzy height of his new life,
May have dethroned the guidance of his mind,
Which might on mother, me, or any one
Vent out its undirected, spleeny thoughts;
Perhaps, though buried in a mint of gold,
He thinks he sees starvation's hungry form;
Or any of the thousand fantasies
That dwelling too much on a single thought
Engenders.

CHARLOTTE.

                    If we should find it so,
How heavenly gentle must our actions be
That we observe no strangeness in his ways;
Attention paying that we disclose not
Our opinion of his infirmity;
For such things surely would increase his mood.

HAROLD.

And we must try by such inventive skill,
As well considered ingenuity
May devise—as lively, entertaining themes,
Laughter, new company, diverting scenes,
The theatre—but not the solemn play—
To tide him from this single rocky reef
Whereon his mind is strand, into the great
And varied sea of thought; not argue him,
For in these one-thought minds, upon their themes

Reason being astray, to reason him
Would be the chief of fallacies.   And next,
It may be possible our father thinks,
And not dishonestly, that our dear mother
Has committed some grave fault, which, perhaps,
May have some slight foundation in the fact.

CHARLOTTE.

If that be so—

HAROLD.

                    The remedy is plain:
Knowing the fault, our mother will amend it.
But there's the last dark inference, that stares
Its monster head aloft above them all.

CHARLOTTE.

Alas! what may that be?

HAROLD.

                    That he has come
To hate our mother—

CHARLOTTE.

            Cruel, cruel thought!

HAROLD.

That in his wealth he longs for some fair one,
Who will to more advantage show him off,
And in a blaze of jewels dazzle out
The eyes of rivalry the world over.

CHARLOTTE.

To doff our mother for a younger wife?
Oh, Heaven defend!   I cannot think so.
I rather would be dead than see that day.

HAROLD.

And so would I—my heart is sick at but
The thought of it.   Yet here our duty rests,
To find the trouble's cause and weed it out;
In this, dear sister, you must be my aid.

CHARLOTTE.

My mind is as your own, and you shall be
The rudder of my acts; but O, dear brother,
Let no mistaken zeal of ours deepen
This trouble and increase our parents' grief,
As ofttimes over-zealousness in children may (*go.
ing*).
O Harold, look, look, where comes the winter
Of our lives, that nine months past we left
In spring!

HAROLD.

O God! my father, it is he.

CHARLOTTE.

See how his form is drooped! how sad his face!

HAROLD.

How slow he walks!   I think that he has aged
Ten years since two days past I saw him here.

CHARLOTTE.

See how he stops, absently pondering!

HAROLD.

Go to him, Charlotte—I in the next room
Will wait—converse with him, then haste to me
And tell me what he says and how he acts.

(*Exit* CHARLOTTE.)

4

Enter HENCHMAN.

HENCHMAN.

Harold, has your father yet returned home?

HAROLD.

Yonder is coming one who might be called
My father.

HENCHMAN.

Indeed, he has been called that.

HAROLD.

Yet one would hardly think him to be such.

HENCHMAN.

Indeed, one might or one might not think so,
And yet to doubt it were a grievous doubt.

HAROLD.

Your speech is too far off; I pray you, sir—

HENCHMAN.

Be more direct and damn myself; speak plain
And be turned out.   Honesty is a fool
That begged, starved, and ended in a gutter
For being too straightforward with his friend.

HAROLD.

If there be any meaning in these words—

HENCHMAN.

Oh, the fickleness of life, of life, and man,
And women, too, for the matter of that!

HAROLD.

By Heaven, you will offend me in this way!

If you have anything to say, speak out.

HENCHMAN.

Oh, be cautious, Harold, be delicate
When you address your stricken father.

HAROLD.

Sir, I shall so address him as becomes
The reverend position that he holds.

HENCHMAN.

Be much more delicate.   If your discourse
Should bear upon his trouble, speak to him
As one in health speaks to a stricken man ;
For trouble makes a kind of wounded mind
That takes offense where no offense is meant.

HAROLD.

I shall in all things guard myself, and give
Offense where nothing but offense should be.

HENCHMAN.

Yet it were best you touch not on his grief.

HAROLD.

Sir, I shall therein be the judge ; good day.

(*Exit* HAROLD.)

HENCHMAN.

Ha ! the villainy of it is too great.
He seemed not to catch my beastly meaning.
It crooks the native straightness of my ways.
I must see Malone and put him on his guard.–
It slimes me over with a filthy coat.--
Money is a friend, money is a friend !

He must not come upon him unaware. –
This money will protect me in my age.
Ha! a thought that might become a monarch!
    (*laughs.*)
What if I, having divorced Malone,
Should marry his widow? Sound old brainpan!
It behooves me now to steer my fragile bark
In the middle of possibilities.
She seems to like me I will think on it.
But she would have no money when divorced.
I might convince Malone––it argues well
It is his moral duty to divide
His money with his wife.–– Sound old brainpan!
Ah! here she comes, and while the notion's on me
I will feel her inclination to me.

    Enter CATHERINE.

CATHERINE.

Doctor, do you know why my husband left?

HENCHMAN.

Alas! dear madam, I am in the dark.

CATHERINE.

I thought, perhaps, that, from your knowledge of
    him,
You might discern the motive of his acts.

HENCHMAN.

True it is that every thought and act
Is fountained in a cause, as true it is
That all the movements of the universe
Are motived in the bosom of sweet nature,

Who sometimes temptingly reveals herself;
But who can grasp the forces infinite
That focus in a sunbeam! So, madam,
Is it with our acts; motives do sometimes
Play upon the face, but sometimes they defy
Our closest scrutiny, laughing to scorn
The efforts of our lawyers and logicians
To uncoil them, and so your husband's seem.

CATHERINE.

But has he not let fall some little word
From which you could discern his conduct's cause?

HENCHMAN.

Your husband is discreet, and knowing well
My oft asserted friendship for his wife
He would be slow to do or say to me
Aught that would cast reproach on you.

CATHERINE.

     Reproach!

I am so ignorant of any cause
Why he should cast reproach on me.

HENCHMAN.

     And I;

Yet there are those who from a lack of cause
Do sometimes cast reproach.

CATHERINE.

     I cannot think

He means me harm.

HENCHMAN.

    Yet by these fiendish acts—

But pardon, madam, I may say too much.
I only say that meaning good and acting bad
Are very distant stars.

CATHERINE.

I am of wives
The most unhappy in this world.   Ah, me!

HENCHMAN.

There, gentle lady, take it not to heart.
Although your husband may dislike you
There is another one esteems you greatly,
Seeing in her whom Edmund so despises
One whose mighty soul is ever filled
With all the virtues of true womanhood.

CATHERINE.

Your kindness twice affects me: I thank you
For your sympathy, yet there are daggers
In it, which make me think that he has said
Much more than you will tell in disrespect of me.

HENCHMAN.

Alas! madam, I fear—yet I would say
No more, lest some unfeeling one might think
I had between a wife and husband gone.

CATHERINE.

A thought so base is foreign to your soul.
And I, who am deprived of him I love,
Appreciate your kindness, though it pain my heart.

HENCHMAN.

Ah, dearest lady, when the heart is robbed

Of that without which it is an aching void,
Sweet nature, by her suffering children pained,
Does seek to fill the chasm with another love.
Ah, lady, how his acts, unhusbandlike,
Inflame my ire, and your too gentle ways
Excite my pity!   Dear madam, I was born
Neath the old *regime*, before the slime of greed
Had blotted out the wealth of chivalry.
Oh, that I might proclaim myself your slave!
Here is my arm; but intimate the thought
And it shall call your husband to account.

CATHERINE.

Oh; no, no, no, oh, no; these savage ways
Cannot bring back his love.

HENCHMAN.

                              Yes, you are right:
The sword is rusty and the pity's great.
There is one only other weapon known—

CATHERINE.

Alas! dear sir, I wish no weapon used.

HENCHMAN.

I mean the dart of love, and you yourself
Must be the archer.   To all his jeers, scoffs,
And acts unhusbandlike, return you naught
But love; which will melt down his icy hate.

CATHERINE.

That will I do, and Heaven grant it be
Sufficient to the end.

HENCHMAN.

I say, Amen.

            (*Exit* CATHERINE.)

When I am rich I'll be the age's beau
And teach these moneyheads the way to woo.
Thus does the devil make good use of saints;
For all the homely love she can pour on him
Is so much fuel to his burning hate.
Still am I slow to take the devil's part,
And were I differently situated
I would not do it.　But here the wronged one
    comes,
And with Charlotte.　I must await near by
And catch his ear before his son comes on him.

            (*Exit* HENCHMAN.)
    Enter MALONE *and* CHARLOTTE.

MALONE.

O, guard it, Charlotte, as you would your life,
And as your hope of Heaven cherish it!

CHARLOTTE.

Dear father, no thought to virtue foreign
Has ever tried the portal of my mind.

MALONE.

It is a diamond of the rarest hue
Set in the forehead of a woman's life;
Alone by which her fairy form is seen,
Which lights her eye, and beautifies her face,
And taken away does leave her but a mass
Black and misshapen.

CHARLOTTE.

But why, dear father,
Do you speak in this strange way?

MALONE.

O Charlotte,
What havoc can a woman make when she goes
  wrong!

CHARLOTTE.

You have some mighty secret on your mind.

MALONE.

Of your companions, too, be very choice.
Contamination breeds by vile companionship,
And chiefly this in women.   I pray you
On these women mark your reprobation;
Such as are basely ignorant avoid;
For knowledge is the forward foot in right,
And ignorance the foremost step in vice.
Such as are frivolous and fast turn from,—
Shun both, and seek the rich companionship
Of those few women, rarest in esteem,
Who, being not stupid, are yet learned,
And being not fast, are yet vivacious.

CHARLOTTE.

These good instructions would be teachers twice
If you will tell me why you give me them.

MALONE.

Go tell your brother Harold I would see him.
                    (*Exit* CHARLOTTE.)
        Enter HENCHMAN *unobserved by* MALONE.

HENCHMAN (*aside*).

When platitudes are not the foods
Of hypocrites, they die of fits.
I'll make my service big. (*Suddenly.*)   Malone,
        Malone!
Are you aware that Harold overheard
You speaking to your wife before you left?

MALONE.

What! No? Is it possible?   I care not,
Being amply justified in what I said.

HENCHMAN.

Why, man—hist! why man you little know
How close you stand upon a lighted mine.
This premature affair has changed the s oul
Of Harold to a boiling spring, that now
Vents forth itself in maledictions fierce,
As it would burst its hold, and then anon
Sinks down, with piteous moan, into his earth
As it would cease to be.

MALONE.

                Poor boy, poor boy!—
Do you know how great I love my children?
Let no consideration rob me of them.
They must be made acquainted, by some means
Sure to convince them, of this woman's guilt.
I pity them as they should pity me.
What is Harold doing? what has he done?

HENCHMAN.

I think he has not slept since *that* occurred.

And all last night he wandered through the park,
Sighing with the trees, and lifting up his soul
In supplication to the Diety
For guidance.

MALONE.

That, you say, he did last night?

HENCHMAN.

As more than once I saw him from my window.

MALONE.

Poor boy! You say you saw him—when I left?

HENCHMAN.

And never looked a being half so piteous.

MALONE.

How looked he, doctor? Did he seem frightened?
Was he startled or angry? How was his face?

HENCHMAN.

It bore the image of profoundest grief.
Under his brow, knit and triangular,
His eyes shown set and lustered like a corpse,
With all his face high ridged and furrowed deep.

MALONE.

You saw him so?

HENCHMAN.

And yet about his mouth
There was a firmness, telling me he could do deeds
Which, at the trying, ordinary mortals fail.

MALONE.

That is very strange, for from his childhood

Harold was wont to be all gentleness.
Touching his ways what else have you observed?

HENCHMAN.

His constant effort to resolve your act.
Questions he every one—his mother, Bourne,
The servants, indirectly, me pointedly—
And I have guarded well your mystery.
Then goes he into theory—this must be,
And then it must be that, then goes again
The whole course, like an imprisoned bird,
Flying from light to light, and still walled in.
But look you, here he comes, and with your wife.
No, foolish man, to go now in their face
Would be conclusive evidence of guilt.

MALONE.

I have more cause than willingness to stay.

HENCHMAN.

That tune is right; maintain it to the end.
                    (*Exit* HENCHMAN.)

MALONE.

How sickly are our wits when we are wrong.
        (*He turns aside so that* HAROLD *and his mother
            enter apparently unobserved by him.*)
        Enter HAROLD *and* CATHERINE.

        CATHERINE (*aside to* HAROLD).

Now, Harold, only by the gentlest means.
No harshness either in your ways or words.

HAROLD.

Nay, mother, have no fear, I will do right.
He seems absorbed, yet I will speak.   Father!

MALONE.

Ah, Harold! very good it seems to me
To have you home again.

HAROLD.

                    And to me, sir,
As you well know, home is that sacred spot
Where Heaven's light illuminates the earth.
I fear you are not well?

MALONE.

                    Indeed, Harold,
I lately have been vexed and much distressed
By mingled cares, which somewhat bear me down.
Of them no more, being life's incidents,
Your coming is the cure of all my woes.
But had I not thought best to sacrifice
The present pleasure to the future good,
Your absence for so long had been unbearable.

HAROLD.

This is the summit of our ethics, sir,
As ofttimes in our family state appears,
When parents for the future of their young
Forego the greener pleasures of the hour.

MALONE.

A happy illustration of my life,
As efforts for your education show.

HAROLD.

For all your kindness and solicitude,
Your sacrifices for your children's sake,
We thank you, father, trusting our efforts
At the schools have been some compensation
For the untiring zeal, forbearance kind, *
And noble generosity of one
Who so desires his family's welfare,
Loving his children with such gentleness.

MALONE.

Yes, Harold, dearly I love my children,
On whose returning love my life depends.
Oh, filial love does to parental love give life,
And dying leaves the universe a void!
Alas! I am grown dotard in this cause.

HAROLD.

Forgive me, father, if the early bloom
Of my young judgment be too forward grown.
But I with larger eyes have come to view
This universe of love, wherein I see
By five ascending plains its fair abode.
The first is blazoned *love of self;* the next
Is mottoed, *love of man and wife;* the third
In golden letters, *here is family love;*
Fourth plain and by the sovereign sculptor carved,
Shines like a throne, *the love of man for man;*
And on the last, in splendid characters,
Here all loves equal meet, but none denied.

MALONE.

Yet mark you, Harold, how the mighty base
Of all our loves is love of self.

HAROLD.

Oh, rather,
Mark you, father, how in each evolving plain
The love of self by loving others is enriched,
And by denying self, self is itself more loved.

MALONE.

Yet all upon the love of self depend.

HAROLD.

No; each on its precedent one depends,
The family, like a pendent world,
Hangs on the happy love of man and wife.

MALONE.

The love of self is as the mighty sun;
All other loves are but his satellites.

HAROLD.

You see this mighty archway of our state,
This splendid firmament of freedom's stars,
This rich society of happy men;
As rests the ponderous mountain on the crust
Of earth, so does our commonwealth repose
Upon the bosom of the family.

MALONE.

Yet rests the family on the love of self.

HAROLD.

Father, you push the love of self too far.
The vast trihedron of connubial love
Is by a triad of affections formed:
That of the husband and the wife for each,

That of the parent and the child for each,
That of the children for one another;
Where these in one harmonious whole exist
They shape the beauteous figure of our family state.
But either side removed, there then remains
Naught but an empty and misshapen thing.

MALONE.

It has greatly pleased me, Harold, thus to test
The depth and compass of your studies ethical.
And, though your reasons somewhat bookish sound,
And smack of inexperience in life,
They show a mind and heart prone to the right.
True, Harold, the family only is
When all its parts in unity accord.

HAROLD.

This is the very essence of our life,
The key-note to existence, and the thing
For which we live.   Here in this charmed abode, -
This little sovereignty where each is sovereign,—
Here burns the lamp that lights the spacious world
Making the dreary earth a fairy land;
Here nations are conceived, empires are born,
And all the dear relationships of life
Bloom like that garden of which poets sing.
Yet mark you, father, this most holy realm
Has laws, which violated taints its blood,
As death converts the perfume of the rose
Into the fetor of decomposition.
The husband or the wife once gone astray

The vulture ruin preys upon the family.
Thus do some children with one parent side,
Some with the other --so divide themselves.
And thus the husband hates the wife, the wife
The husband, the husband the following
Of the wife, and the wife the following
Of the husband, the children the parents
Whom they follow not, and they each other
Who go not together; and so the heavens
A hell become, and pandemonium reigns.

MALONE. ·

Pleased am I, Harold, thus to see how you
Have learned the ethics of the family.

HAROLD.

Why how sweet it is, how like to Heaven,
How God-appointed this relationship!
Behold it in the stages of its life:
At first a man and woman, young in years,
Upon the very threshold of existence,
Neither with worldly goods, experience, nor aught
Save love and willingness, so join their lives;
Then in their being comes the second period,
When their united strength wages fierce combat
Against the world's poverty and hardship;
During which time, most like, and, as it were,
Springing from their beings, baptized by their
United love, to the world they give new lives.
Third stage arrives when they have struck the
    middle
Of their lives, and fortune's slow creeping form

Has overtaken them.   Surrounded now
With all the luxuries of wealth, loving
Each other, by their children idolized—

CATHERINE.

How sweet the picture to my longing eyes!

HAROLD.

Then comes the last, when children's children
Carry them to their very marriage,
Making them live their past lives o'er again,
Stripped of all hardships and privations.

MALONE.

A life of such rare, wondrous happiness
Makes immortality begin on earth.

HAROLD.

Yes, so it does.   But here I have o'erreached
Your patience, and as a youthful playwright
Does moralize his play away, so I
With too much ethics have damped the pleasure
Of our meeting.   Have you seen Richard, sir?

MALONE.

No, Harold, nor yet seen Helen either.

HAROLD.

How selfish in me! let me go and fetch them.

> (*Exit* HAROLD. *He at once returns and
> secretes himself behind a screen, but in
> view of the audience.*)

CATHERINE (*timidly*).

Husband, I have much regretted—

MALONE.

Indeed!
Oh, wondrous mind that can at least regret!
Watch your conscience and remorse may follow.

CATHERINE.

Edmund, my conscience has no stain upon it.

MALONE.

Eternal Justice, listen! What, no stain?
How have you washed it in these two days past?

CATHERINE.

By searching it for any spot of wrong
Toward you, husband.

MALONE.

Oh, specious pretext!
Go fling it in the sea and let the waves
Attempt its cleansing.

CATHERINE.

Alas! I would that I
Were there, but for my children and God's laws.
What crime has my poor soul been guilty of?
Is it my love for you? If that be so
I will curb in the outward show of it,
And with it unexpressed be satisfied.
Is it the plainness of my face? I will
With all the woman's art enliven it.

MALONE.

O woman, for the love of mercy, peace!

CATHERINE.

Nay, husband, of my offense inform me.
Is it my education's poverty,
My lack of words, of grace and nimble ways?
I will be mastered, booked, and learn to trip
And talk and amble with a lady's mien.

MALONE.

Court you hatred?   Go to your priest and learn
To there unlearn the vileness you have taught
   yourself.

CATHERINE (*with emphasis*).

Edmund, for Heaven's love, renounce those words.

MALONE.

Go find a place, if there be such on earth,
Where goodness counts not, and there hide your
   face.

CATHERINE.

Sweet Heaven, give me patience, give me patience.
There is an end, an end, an end, O Father!

                    (*Exit* CATHERINE.)

          (HAROLD *comes forward.*)

MALONE.

O Harold!

HAROLD.

              Peace to your soul's alarm!
For this unmannered watch, I pardon beg;
My love must furnish forth its good excuse.
I have not stayed to quarrel with you, sir.

MALONE.

O Harold, I am weary of this life,
Which slowly drags its freighted weight along
Over the dreary world to immortality.

HAROLD.

Now, father, what great gulf is this between you
And my mother?

MALONE.

   The words would burn my tongue,
That named them to you, Harold.

HAROLD.

     And must I,
Who am the very growth, the primal limb,
Of this most sacred trunk, be quite cut off,
Denied all intercourse, and left to die?

MALONE.

I cannot speak; my heart and yours would break.
There is no justice in this world for me.

HAROLD.

No justice?—here on my knees—witness God!—
Here I proclaim myself—if you are wronged
And she prove obdurate—forever hence
Upon your side demanding equity.
Make me to see the stain of which you spoke,
And here I swear into the raging sea
To fling my love, and live for only you.

MALONE.

Have patience, son, crime will reveal itself.

HAROLD.

By our common love I implore you.

MALONE.

No.

HAROLD.

By our common faith I entreat you.

MALONE.

No.

HAROLD.

By the right of a son I demand it;
For the love of your wife deny me not;
For your children's sake, if you love them.

MALONE.

No.

HAROLD.

For the sake of mankind —

MALONE.

No, Harold, no.

HAROLD (*rising*).

Then you love us none, but in the iron cloak
Of self ensheathe your adamantine soul,
Loving not God, nor man, nor wife, nor child,
Nor anything except your stolid self.

MALONE.

O Harold, you have hereby pierced my heart,
And I have lived too long when thus my child
Demands a warrant for his father's death!

Alas, for life when life is so awry!

> (*He sinks into a chair, covering his face with
> his hands, and pretends to weep.*)

HAROLD (*aside*).

Cruelty is herein merciful; and,
Though it break my own, I will unseal his heart.—
Sir, in my conduct's eye throughout my life
I have beheld you on that majestic throne,
That splendid station that a father fills.

MALONE.

One might well doubt I were your father
To hear you so upbraid me.

HAROLD.

Indeed, sir,
One might well doubt you were my father
To hear you so upbraid my mother;
For, if you were my father, surely you
Would more the husband of my mother be.

MALONE.

God grant that blow may ne'er return on you.

HAROLD.

You cannot thwart me by this subtle mien.
The star of husband-fatherhood that burned
In the zenith of my love has fallen.
I have seen my gracious mother beg you,
I have on my lowly knees implored you,
For that the docked criminal of right may have
And justice to her meanest felon ne'er denies.

What pitiful offense is this that lives on sighs,
And dares not breathe in words!   E'en were she
    wrong,
And triple-plated justice on your side,
A prosecution by such cruel means
Would to a persecution change, the crime
In the complainant growing greatest.

MALONE.

Is it for this that I have all my life
In the hot caverns of the earth delved down,
On frozen summits worked, in deserts lived,
Foregone all pleasures, for my children's sake,
And chiefly you?   O you fathers, hear me
To the world's remotest ends, never more
For your children labor, never more love them!

HAROLD.

There is the curse, the very curse of it,
That any father should so love his son
And with such rancor hate the mother of that son!
Sure you are sane, which doubted I at first,
For on all other themes you reason right,
And monomania upon its fancied wrongs
Would harp, where you keep closely prisoned mind;
And surely you have no just cause for blame
Against your wife, or you would make that known.
But mark you how betwixt the real ground
And fancied cause, stands up the crooked form,
Sighing, yet tongueless, of hypocritic pretense!
What! is the glass so perfect that you see

The ghost of your own skeleton?   Why, sir,
The air is reeky with the news—it stinks
In the nose of every beldam gossip
On the Coast, that shortly you shall put away
Your wife and take a fresher one!

MALONE.

O God!

HAROLD.

O God, say I!—what! are you blind?   See there
Where on her knees, the crucifix in hand—
Dare you not look?—my mother does implore
Divinity to save her from this outrage.

MALONE.

Well, have you done?

HAROLD.

Your calmness comes too late.

The verdict, not the prison, makes the guilty quake.
Alas! what monstrous crime is this, that from
The due obedience of a loving son
Converts me to a gross accuser of my sire?

MALONE.

Deeper remorse than this may seize you yet.

HAROLD.

To barter off my mother and your wife
For such a twittering, painted, pasty,
Hair-be-frizzled dot as underneath the name
Of beauty sails in the air of our society!

MALONE.

O Harold, you are deaf to your own words!

HAROLD.

To fling your fair name into the foul stench
Of the public slaughter-house!—

MALONE.

No more of this.

HAROLD.

To drag your children through the filthy slums
That a proceeding such as this must make!
And all for what?   To bask for a brief day
In the bought smiles of a purchased bride,
Reek in the mulching of a fickle bed,
Gape when she ambles in another's arms,
And have the staring multitude cry, *Lo,*
How beautiful a wife he has!

MALONE.

Harold!

HAROLD.

Beauty—the saying rusts—is but skin deep.
Note you the proof: Here is the slab; here lies
The form and face of Venus; this is the knife
And mine the hungry student's hand.   An hour—
Not half so long—the skin of beauty's stripped!
See those eyes, which once like sparkling diamonds
Had lit up the night, now bulging out
Like two disgusting warts—beautiful eyes!
And that nose, that chiseled piece of marble,
See! 'tis a pretty piece of gristle now.
And those tinted cheeks—yes, and that dimpled
    chin—

Why, sir, they are naught but rapes of raw meat.
And all those veins, which gave Aurora's color
To the face, are streaks of clotted gore.
Ah, but those lips, for but one kiss from which
You might have squandered half a fortune,
Are taut upon the teeth drawn back into a grin
Ghastly as death itself!   Do you now know
In what great depths the seat of beauty lies ?
And would you of it rather be possessed
Than that impenetrable honor and virtue
Which not a surgeon's knife can cut away

MALONE.

O Harold, you have frozen up my veins!

HAROLD.

Go warm them, father, at my mother's heart.
Renounce this most unworthy scheme, and I
In ashes will repent what I have said.

MALONE.

This scheme is but the vintage of your mind.

HAROLD.

Let us not bandy words,—say it is so,
Which Heaven grant it is.   But, father, go,
A decent pardon of my mother beg,
And set her heart to rights; or, if that be
More than you think your dignity becomes,
Promise me this, that you will now put off
This most mysterious demeanor,
And treat your wife in all things as becomes
The lofty station of a wife and mother.

MALONE.

My treatment shall accord with her deserts.

HAROLD.

Why, that's to say you will not change your ways.

MALONE.

You know not what you ask.   If you were me
You would behold her through another eye.

HAROLD.

What hellish she has caught you in her web
That you to honor, duty, family, are dead?
Come, look you on this scene: Here is your home—
The honored end of more than half a life--
A domicile to house a prince, a fort
Enclosing love; here is your wife, and she,
With you, the joint producer of your wealth.
Here are your children, entails of your name!
A future that might dazzle monarchs' eyes!
Now look on that: There is your house, not home,
Blazed with the gaudy trappings of the hour;
Your mistress there, pampered and puffed like sin,
Decked in the gross embellishments of new reaped
        wealth,
The magpie gossip of society.
Childless you must remain, or children have
That bear the mark of doubtful parentage,
For we discarded offspring will with mother go.
Now what is this to that ?   Home to brothel,
Wife to bawd, love to lust, reality
To myth, and decency to vanity.

In Heaven's name what betterment can hope sug-
 gest
To make you plunge from this fair paradise
To that foul hell?

MALONE.

    You prattle idly.

HAROLD.

Prattle! call you this prattle? Then, if you will,
Crack up this little world. against the wall
Of justice fling yourself. I in the breach
Will guard my mother's rights; but press me not
Too far, or else these hands—

MALONE.

    Harold, my son!

HAROLD.

Yes, these very hands may not remember
That you are the father.

MALONE.

   The day shall come—

HAROLD.

When my dear mother's rights are sacredly ob
 served.

MALONE.

When you shall beg upon your bended knees—

HAROLD.

Yes, and implore your wronged wife's mercy.

MALONE.

For this unkindness my forgiveness, son.

HAROLD.

Forgiveness! and adds hypocrisy to crime!

(*Exit* HAROLD.)

Enter HENCHMAN.

Well done, Malone, marvelously well done.
From yonder room I have observed it all.
You waste your genius; turn actor and play
The part of Tartuffe.

MALONE.

You will oblige me
By maintaining toward me in my grief
A changed and more respectful demeanor.

HENCHMAN.

Good, by Jupiter, excellently well!
(*Aside*) A monkey playing a Jew's-harp.

MALONE.

Henchman!

HENCHMAN.

Ay, sir—as one should say in tragedy.

MALONE.

Have you no heart?

HENCHMAN.

One somewhat stuffed with brains.

MALONE.

No feeling?

HENCHMAN.

Oh! I am all emotion

Shall I quiver?

MALONE.

No more of this, I say.

HENCHMAN.

Why, bless my life, Malone, are you in earnest?

MALONE.

Is it the proper thing to sport with one
Whose wife has played him false?

HENCHMAN.

Why, now, that's so.
Ah, thoughtless me! forgive me, dear Malone.

MALONE.

Alas! I fear my son has gone from me.

HENCHMAN.

Fear not, these things are providential.

MALONE.

I cannot see them so.

HENCHMAN.

This way, mark you;
The human mind is like a metal spring,
The harder it is struck, being not snapped,
The greater will the rebound be. So 'tis
With Harold, whose elastic mind
Has by the ponderous and depressing blow
Of your *apparent* villainy been struck.
Now, when he sees you are the injured one,
The weight being removed, he will fly back to you
With all his nature's fierce impetuosity.

MALONE.

Your jerky style imports a labored reason.
I pray it may be so, yet greatly fear.

(*Exit* MALONE.)

HENCHMAN.

He *prays* it may be so ! he prays ! he prays !
　　　　　(*As though praying to the devil.*)
O sweety devil, holy devil,
Most pure devil, hear my supplication !
I'll turn a praying, too, if this continue long,
It is such mirth to mock the hypocrite.

Enter CATHERINE.

CATHERINE.

O sir, my troubles are grown mountain high.
Harold has but increased his father's wrath,
Who, by insinuations deep, attempts
To turn my children from me.

HENCHMAN.
　　　　　　　　Dear lady,
What nature has these *vile* insinuations ?

CATHERINE.

Alas ! they take no form.

HENCHMAN.
　　　　　　　　They therefore are
More dangerous.　An open charge is like
A lion; it may at least be fought,
But innuendoes are those subtle germs,
Unseen, ungraspable, yet deadly, which slyly
Creep into the body of a reputation,

Which ere we know it dies.   O dear lady,
These innuendoes are very poison
To your children's love—we must unearth their
    cause.

CATHERINE.

Ah me! where shall I go for other help?
Since you and Harold fail, I have lost heart.

HENCHMAN.

In all my feeble efforts in your dear behalf
There has appeared before my watchful eyes
The name of Maurice Bourne.   *Sure*, I have said,
These men having for more than half a life
Been close companions, if your husband gave
His confidence to any one, that one is Bourne.

CATHERINE.

I, too, have thought of Maurice, and ofttimes
Have pricked my courage on to tell him.
But, oh, the shame of it!—to have him know
There is between myself and Edmund trouble;
Besides it ill becomes my wifely modesty.

HENCHMAN.

Modesty, and all her lovely sisterhood,
Good madam, live in the mind, intention
Being their very gist, substance and all.
And when the heart is pure, the showy forms
And outward manners of its tenement
Are quite indifferent; but when the mind
Is soiled by evil thoughts, no etiquette
Can purify the act; and what without

A cause is gross indecency, becomes,
When with a reason coupled, sweetest modesty;
Therefore with a pure heart go to your friend,
And lay your cause before him from the first.

CATHERINE.

Knowing I mean but good I will see Maurice.

HENCHMAN.

Kind Heaven grant your cause prosperity.
Where will you see him, madam?

CATHERINE.

                    In this room,
The parlor, sitting room, or any place.

HENCHMAN.

What if your husband should o'erhear you?

CATHERINE.

I know not how it might affect him.

HENCHMAN.

There it is, madam; our worthiest acts
Have this complexion; that howsoever good
They be we should so do them as to bring no ill.
We must be very prudent in our cause,
For if your husband knew of your intent
To query out the meaning of his acts
It might increase his wrath. Therefore, meet Bourne
At some place where your husband may not see
      you.

CATHERINE.

By your wise counsel will I be advised.
What place would you suggest?

HENCHMAN.

               Now let me see.—
There is a place about the center of the park,
Close to the flower house, where a live oak
Uplifts its canopy to shade the light.
There ofttimes I have whiled the night away
In solitary thoughts on immortality.
It is a holy spot where anciently
Old Father Serra blessed the Indians.
There, madam, is the place to meet your friend.

CATHERINE.

I will do so.

HENCHMAN.

         'Twere better done at once.
I will invite your friend.   At eight o'clock?

CATHERINE.

As you advise. Kind Heaven grant the end
May justify the means.

HENCHMAN.

         Madam, amen.
               (*Exit* CATHERINE.)
The devil is master of ceremonies.

   Enter GLASCO.

Now who's his dignity? That is the remnant
of a phiz that I have somewhere seen.

GLASCO.

This is the fellow of whom Malone spoke. ¡I must impress him. (*With dignity.*) Good evening, sir.

HENCHMAN (*imitating* GLASCO).

Good evening, sir.

GLASCO.

A pleasant evening, sir.

HENCHMAN.

A pleasant evening, sir.

GLASCO.

I presume this is Doctor Henchman.

HENCHMAN.

I presume this is Doctor Henchman.

GLASCO.

I hope you are well, sir.

HENCHMAN.

I hope you are well, sir.

GLASCO.

I perceive you are from the South, sir.

HENCHMAN.

I perceive you are from the South, *sir.*

GLASCO.

Have you been out here long?

HENCHMAN.

'49er.　Have you been out here long?

GLASCO.

I came in '50.

HENCHMAN.

Where did you stop?

GLASCO.

At—er—at Old Calamity Hill.   Where did you
stop?

HENCHMAN.

At—er—at Old Calamity Hill.   Sir, your face
has a distantly familiar contortion about it; and
having run the parrot gamut of greeting, may
I have the honor to know your name?

GLASCO.

My name is Glasco, William Glasco, attorney-at-
law, of San Francisco.

HENCHMAN.

Glasco? Glasco?

GLASCO.

Glasco, sir.

HENCHMAN

And you came here in '49?

GLASCO.

In '50, sir.

HENCHMAN.

What was your name then?

GLASCO.

Sir?

HENCHMAN.

Beg pardon, but a name is such a help to memory. Glasco? Glasco?—Coglass!

GLASCO.

Sir?

HENCHMAN.

What! Bill Coglass who ran a faro game in Jim McCrackin's saloon?

GLASCO.

Sir, I understand—

HENCHMAN.

But I don't, how you are now Judge Glasco, the famous lawyer of San Francisco.

GLASCO.

Sir, I understand that you are a witness in a certain case, that Mr. Malone is shortly to bring against his—er—er—against his—er.

HENCHMAN.

Er—er—mother-in-law.

GLASCO.

I have heard Malone speak very highly of you.

HENCHMAN.

As he might speak of his dog! Thus, he scents well; is an excellent retriever; will follow or go before as you like; will not bark when he should keep still,—a most excellent cur, that will do for his food what his master will have him do!

GLASCO.

I have not heard him speak of you in this regard.

HENCHMAN.

Oh, the shame of it, Glasco, the shame of it, that we who have the brains must play the lackey's part to they who have the wealth! Are we lawyers? for their retainers we corrupt our judgments; Judges? for their influence we murder justice; legislators? for their bribes we make the laws they ask; editors? for their subsidies they hold our pens; preachers? for pew rent we give our consciences to the devil—and all for what? A night's lodging and a full belly!

GLASCO.

Tut, tut! I have heard him praise you as a most excellent and trustworthy gentleman.

HENCHMAN.

I had rather he had damned me for a common bawd. For I have fallen down so low beneath my own contempt that I have nothing left—except a tongue to own my villainy and make a sport of hypocrites.

GLASCO.

I know nothing of this.

HENCHMAN.

Bah! Your nose is so used to the stench it fails to notice it. Most righteous and clear-conscienced,

my very dear sir Lawyer, what would you with me?
Drop slabbering and come to terms.

Glasco.

I understand you are working up this case?

Henchman.

Well, yes; I am looking after Malone's matrimonial interests.

Glasco.

Now, I understand that his wife and one Bourne have been guilty of—

Henchman.

O Lord, yes; you can see them any day in each other's arms—on the street, in the theater, in church. Oh! believe me, they're a vile lot.

Glasco.

Well, sir, I will tell you what evidence I want and you will get it.

Henchman.

I will? Would you prefer that I should make or buy it?

Glasco.

No, sir; you shall *find* it.

Henchman.

Tweedle dum and tweedle dee. Well, what evidence shall I find for your purity?

GLASCO.

Circumstantial evidence of matrimonial incontinency.

HENCHMAN.

B-a-n-g; and yet there is a short way of calling that bang! I have run ahead of you and announced you to my lady. What you mean is that you want me to *find* witnesses who will swear—

GLASCO.

Pardon me, sir; a lawyer never cares to go too minutely into such things. All I ask is evidence showing that these parties had a previous liking for each other, clandestine correspondence, stolen interviews, passionate declarations, and the opportunity for the consummation of the offense.

HENCHMAN.

You have no doubt of the veritable existence of such evidence?

GLASCO.

Sir, the lawyer tries his case on the evidence submitted to him; the truthfulness of the evidence is a matter for the witness.

Enter MALONE.

MALONE.

Gentlemen, this is a very sad occasion.

GLASCO.

A very sad one, indeed, sir.

HENCHMAN.

A very sad one, indeed, sir.

GLASCO.

May I speak with you in private, Malone?

(*Exit* MALONE *and* GLASCO.)

HENCHMAN.

By Heavens, I am the only villain!
Enrobe a crime in lawyers' gowns and it
Becomes a virtue ; dress lawyers' virtue
In laymen's rags and it becomes a crime.
O virtuous, sweet, clear-conscienced villain,
O law-protected villain, fare thee well!
So are we all villains in our way.

(*Exit* HENCHMAN.)

ACT III.

SCENE.—MALONE'S *country place; a park with a flower house; night.*

Enter HENCHMAN *and* GLASCO.

HENCHMAN.

I am no lawyer such as you are, sir,
Versed in the labyrinths of legal lore,
But with a wider compass of my eye
Review this mater of divorce.   I see
A man and woman married, but I see
Him grown to hate, despise and loathe his wife.
She, we will say, is virtuous and good—
Gives him no legal cause for a divorce.

GLASCO.

Of this I know, and care to know, nothing.

HENCHMAN.

Well, well; you prattle with a lawyer's tongue.
The vinculum of marriage here is broke,
Yet the law affords the husband no relief.

GLASCO.

The lawyer will, if you do well your part.

HENCHMAN.

Yes, but that slimes the majesty of law.
And yet, Glasco, the fault lies in the law,
Which ofttimes turns the hangman of itself,
When to a climax of ideal life
It tries to force our human natures.

GLASCO (*aside*).

Tiresome fool!—But, sir, with the policy
Of laws the advocate has naught to do.
To evade the bad laws and to enforce
Such as are good is the lawyer's business.

HENCHMAN (*half abstractedly*).

Something is rotten in the policy
Of laws which force us mortals through a course
Of villainy to reach our native rights (*pauses*).

GLASCO (*aside*).

The old fish is hooked, but must play it out
Ere I can land him.

HENCHMAN.

                    These serving laws,—
Vain hour-long flatterers!—tickle the consciences
That they seduce, then serve to bribe our courts,
Corrupt our juries, perjure our witnesses,
Convert our lawyers into tricksters vile,
And turn the native current of our acts
Out from the channel of its probity.
There's something rotten in our statute of divorce.

GLASCO (*impatiently*).

But to this case.

HENCHMAN (*suddenly*).

But to this case, indeed;
And the problem is, to win or not to win.
I would compare a lawyer's duty thus:
Positive win, comparative wind,
Superlative wind.

GLASCO (*aside*).

Ha! a razor tongue.

HENCHMAN.

I would I knew the tricks of your trade, for I suppose there is scarce one chance in a dozen for a shrewd lawyer to lose a case, however bad it be.

GLASCO (*aside*).

He floats where I would have him.—Well, doctor, as to that, there are, betwixt the beginning and the ending of a bad law suit, many steps, appeals, and chances not mentioned in the codes.

HENCHMAN.

Indeed!

GLASCO.

And as we are about to undertake a case of vast importance—

HENCHMAN.

Wherein there must be tricks or no tricks.

GLASCO.

You may as well be made acquainted with these—

HENCHMAN.

Eccentricities of your profession.

GLASCO.

Still, you must know that I have learned these things by observation, not experience.

HENCHMAN.

Ah! it flies without wings. It is too bad that such a dear young innocent as you are should be set down unprotected in this immoral world, and how odd it is that 'mongst the dirty clothes of your trade you have kept your own linen so unspotted! But pardon me, let the magician begin his tricks—from faro to law is but a step.

GLASCO (*aside*).

I must bear with him.—First, at the doorway of your suit lies your pocket appeal to the virtuous judge to quash the case. Your second step is a money application to the witnesses against you. Third chance is to manufacture witnesses out of coin. Fourth resort is a pocket appeal to the virtuous sheriff to procure a jury of your inclining. Fifth step is at the door of honest jurymen. Sixth effort is a lucre application to the conscientious judge to undo what has gone before. Last effort, and by its nature topping all, is your appeal to the Court Supreme, where, I have heard, the sack is at times a great argument.

HENCHMAN.

In the lovely name of Justice, do you lawyers do such things?

GLASCO.

A villainous, beastly presumption !

HENCHMAN.

Then, since your holiness does them not, who does them ?

GLASCO.

Your client; or, if he be troubled with a tender conscience, he get some—particular—friend—to do them.

HENCHMAN.

And therein lies the point; when the lawyer winks, the client buys; when the client squirms, the Henchman's turn arrives.

Enter CATHERINE *at a distance diffidently.*

Hist ! the devil is abroad to-night—get behind that tree or he will catch you.

GLASCO.

Here, indeed, is the beginning of a case.

HENCHMAN.

Out of which a pettifogger, or great lawyer, might make something.

GLASCO.

What does she here ?

HENCHMAN.

The devil knows, but may take his imp into confidence.

CATHERINE.

How dark it seems,—this is the place he named.

GLASCO.

Remember that.

HENCHMAN.

That's food for juror's brains.

CATHERINE.

Why does he not come?

GLASCO.

Mark that! set it down.

Enter BOURNE *at a distance.*

The paramour! —a circumstance, indeed.

HENCHMAN.

Yonder is more fortune—Harold, ghost-like,
Stalking among the trees; quick, get away,
And I will bring him within range of them.

GLASCO.

Proof to convict a saint; be cautious, sir.

(*Exeunt* HENCHMAN *and* GLASCO.)

CATHERINE (*seeing* BOURNE).

Maurice, my old friend!

BOURNE.

Nay, but what is this?
What mean these broken words?

CATHERINE.

A broken heart.

BOURNE.

Sure this is strange! Why must we, who have been
Friends for more than twenty years, now meet,
Like outlaws, here in this clandestine way?

CATHERINE.

Do not chide me, Maurice.

BOURNE.

Chide you, for what?

CATHERINE.

My husband hates me!

BOURNE.

In Heaven's name, for what?

Enter HAROLD *and* HENCHMAN. (BOURNE
and CATHERINE *continue their conversa-
tion in a low tone.*)

HENCHMAN.

What think you of Kant's *Critique*, my young
friend?

HAROLD.

Some other time, if it please you, Doctor.
Now, as to this estrangement between
My father and my mother, have you seen—

HENCHMAN.

The book is an excellent subtlety—

HAROLD.

Please you, sir, speak of my parents' troubles.

HENCHMAN.

Harold, I rather would not mention them.
I am here in dual state, as doctor
And as guest; either one should seal my lips.

HAROLD.

But you know, Doctor, I have been absent.

HENCHMAN.

And I am sorry I have been present.
I pray you, let us speak no more on this.

HAROLD.

But can you form no notion of the cause?
Has not some word or act disclosed its source?

HENCHMAN.

Our married lives are full of small discords,
Which night, Nature's blest court of equity
Adjusting, tunes to sweeter harmony.
But there are acts which soil and stain the face
Of decency, and crimson modesty.

HAROLD.

Why, now, you make me think some such is here.

(HENCHMAN *jumps quickly in front of* HAR-
OLD, *and between him and where* CATH-
ERINE *and* BOURNE *are standing.*)

HENCHMAN.

Oh! look you yonder where the silver queen,

Rising above the summit of the range,
Unveils the night and throws a million kisses
To the sleeping world.

HAROLD.

Why, what startled you?

HENCHMAN.

Nothing, I think, unless the queenly kiss
Awaked my amorous love of nature.

HAROLD.

Why jumped you so before me? even now
Your actions are as frightened as a deer's.

HENCHMAN.

And see; how every leaf becomes an eye!

HAROLD.

Doctor, do you see those people yonder?
Is the park become a lovers' hiding-place?

HENCHMAN.

Lovers, Harold?—lovers!—nay, watch them not,
They are but some strollers wandered this way.

HAROLD.

Strollers, say you? why, that's like my mother,
Else am I blind; is that not Maurice Bourne?

HENCHMAN.

Bourne! your mother! Look what you say, Harold!
Think you they would be here at such an hour?
I think your mother's virtue is too strong.

HAROLD.

My mother's virtue is as strong as steel.—
I see but illy, yet it must be them.

HENCHMAN.

No, Harold, your mother would not—could not—
Come, come, look on no more; let us go back.

HAROLD.

Nay, tug not so; I would see who they are.

HENCHMAN.

See no more;—the air is chilly, sir.
Let us go back; this thing you see is naught,
Your mother has not so lost her virtue—
'Tis but your fancy.

HAROLD.

         Let me go, Henchman.
See, it is they!

HENCHMAN.

     Go back! go back! go back!

HAROLD.

Go back!—to hell, go back! Your go-backs"mean
Much more than mere go-back—I will not go.
Look, she entreats him with outstretched arms,
   hark!
Their voices rise, listen!

CATHERINE.

        Oh, no, Maurice!
Tell me not it is another woman—
Anything but that.

HENCHMAN.

   Maybe she upbraids him

For some other woman.

    (*Exeunt* CATHERINE *and* BOURNE.)

    HAROLD.

      I will kill you.

    HENCHMAN.

I only said, it may be, not it is.

They have heard you and moved away.

    HAROLD (*impetuously*).

        Henchman,

Tell me the truth of this—if you but swerve

A hair's breadth on either side of fact,

May you be damned!   Is this a common thing?

    HENCHMAN.

Tut! Harold, speak not this way.   She is your—

    HAROLD.

Give me the truth direct—slur not a fact—

    HENCHMAN.

Why, why!

    HAROLD.

   Nor exculpate—

    HENCHMAN.

      Am I a child

To be frightened into telling truth?

    HAROLD.

Oh, if you love justice, speak, Henchman, speak!

HENCHMAN.

Take you me to be the retail merchant
Of all the gossip in the neighborhood?

HAROLD.

In Heaven's name, have you seen this thing before?

HENCHMAN.

It is not for me to say, nor will I.

HAROLD.

I beg you tell me—she is my mother.

HENCHMAN.

I would rather be a snake and half my life
Live coiled up dead than be the trumpeter
Of every bastard rumor to which
The pregnant air gives birth. I will not say.

HAROLD.

O God, this is the lightning's flash that brings
To sight the black night of my father's deeds,
And in a minute blazes forth their cause !

HENCHMAN.

This may be but an aberration, sir.

HAROLD.

Keep such sophistry for unread jurors.—
If 'twere by itself it might be innocent;
Joined with my father's acts it grows a crime.

HENCHMAN.

It were best you think on this theme no more.

HAROLD.

Then I shall cease to think.

HENCHMAN.

If of her guilt
Or innocence you would be quite convinced,
Await developments.

HAROLD.

Ask me to wait
The development of ruin, the world's end.

HENCHMAN.

But, Harold, it may not yet have come to—

HAROLD.

Chaos, desolation, the rot of time.

HENCHMAN.

What we have seen with doubtful eyes may be
But the appearance of unchastity.

HAROLD.

Ha! look how you speak ! she is my mother.

HENCHMAN.

Now you speak right, and like a loving son.
To basely say your mother is guilty
When she but seems to be so, is to wrong her,
Wrong your father, and, more, to wrong yourself.
It is sure a crime to lay a baseless charge
Of foul unchastity on any woman.
How monstrous then becomes the crime when
    laid
On your before-thought virtuous mother.

HAROLD.

Out on this seeming ! all the smooth words
In Italy could only gloss this foulness.
The world is a huge graveyard, and women
Are but walking skeletons of sin,
That need the lightning's flash to bare their bones.—
This must be so.   O Atlantean shoulders
That must pack this world unto my father.

(Exit HAROLD.)

HENCHMAN.

I like not this business—it grows too serious·
Had I seen its end, I had not begun it.   I'll have
no more to do with it.   I'll wash my hands of it.
I'll go on the woman's side and show these devils
up.   Then I'll not get the money.—What if I get
the money?   Yes, but what if I get in jail for
getting it, and what if I get in hell for false swear-
ing?   I'll not do't—it's not right—Higho, Henchman ! whence this spasm of your conscience?

A VOICE.

Conscience !

HENCHMAN.

Ha! ha! who said conscience?

A VOICE.

Hell!

HENCHMAN.

Ha! ha! who said hell?

A VOICE.

Right!

HENCHMAN.

Ha! ha! who said right?

A VOICE.

Wrong!

HENCHMAN.

Ha! ha! who said wrong? And yet I do not this business from the pure love of wrong.

A VOICE.

Wrong!

HENCHMAN.

Damn the word! Wrong? What's wrong? What's right? What's hell? What's conscience? There you are, old Conscience, there you are, old Devil, ever bobbing up before me arguing your sides. By Jupiter, I'll hold a court and pass judgment on this case! Right and Wrong shall be the litigants; old Conscience and the Devil, lawyers; Henchman, the Judge.

(A white form suddenly appears on one side, and a black form on the other side of HENCHMAN.*)**

Wrong, *alias* Henchman, *vs.* Right, *alias* Hench-

---

*To justify the introduction of these "forms," I am constrained to violate the rule which requires that the drama should be self-explanatory. There is a species of hallucination, to which even the soundest minds are at times subject, whereby the person sees, in a shadowy sort of way, forms and images, which are, of course, but the embodiment of his own thoughts. While under the influence of such a spell, the holding of imaginary conversations with such forms is not uncommon. The scene thereby created, is, I think, a proper subject for the drama; not because it has any existence, in fact, but because while it exists it is a reality to the one who thinks he sees it; and the only way to appreciate a character is to translate one's self into his position and condition.

man's conscience.   Are you ready for the plaintiff?

BLACK FORM.

Please, your honor, I ask for a continuance.

HENCHMAN.

There you are, old pettifogger, always asking for a continuance.   What'll you do for a continuance at the day of Judgment.   You'll take out your continuance in purgatory.   You can delay this case no longer.   Ready for the defendant ?

WHITE FORM.

Ready, your honor.

HENCHMAN.

Then at it, and damn formalities.

WHITE FORM.

It is not right that you should break this family up.

HENCHMAN.

There you are, old Conscience, always speaking first.   The plaintiff should begin.

BLACK FORM.

This family has fallen apart of its own weight; it is not your honor does it.

HENCHMAN.

Good point—well said—old Devil.

WHITE FORM.

This is a shallow subterfuge.

BLACK FORM.

At least it is Malone and not your honor breaks
it up.

WHITE FORM.

Your honor is a party to the act, and violates the
rule infallible of right.

HENCHMAN.

What say you to that, Mr. Devil? Is there a
rule infallible of right?

BLACK FORM.

Aye, one that changes with the moon, or each
new edict of the church, or roams about following
the whims of legislators, or spies itself in each
fresh custom of society, or else, barring all these,
lives in a caldron of well boiled reptiles.

(*Laughs sardonically.*)

WHITE FORM.

I'll not argue with such a liar.

HENCHMAN.

What, old Conscience, back out in this way?
Come, at the devil in his own style.

WHITE FORM.

It is not my way. Your honor has allowed your
love of money to bribe your better self.

HENCHMAN.

Thou liest, Conscience! It is not my love o
money, but my hate of poverty.

BLACK FORM (*aside*).

When the judge takes up the lawyer's side the lawyer may retire.

WHITE FORM (*faintly*).

I pray, your honor, do not let the devil rule you.

HENCHMAN.

What, old barrister, your voice is almost out of hearing.

WHITE FORM (*louder*).

If you do this act, I'll set a raging war agoing in you.

BLACK FORM.

He tries to scare you.

WHITE FORM.

I'll pinch you in a thousand places.

BLACK FORM.

He tries to scare you.

WHITE FORM.

I'll rack you with remorse.

BLACK FORM.

He tries to scare you.

WHITE FORM.

I'll put you in the company of thieves.

BLACK FORM.

He tries to scare you.

HENCHMAN.

Order in this Court !

WHITE FORM.

I'll make you hold your head down, so you'll not dare to look at honest men.

HENCHMAN.

Thou liest !

BLACK FORM.

He tries to scare you.

WHITE FORM.

I'll damn your soul in hell.

BLACK FORM.

H e tries to scare you.

HEN CHMAN.

Out on you both ! I'll have no more of you. This Court's adjourned. (*Forms vanish.*) The devil take me if I ever hold another Court like that ! Why this is slinking dotage. It grows late, and it grows late with me. Pure fear, pure fear !— Whoever called me coward ? Oh, I'll do't, I'll do't ! —the job is more than half done now. I think I see me in mine ease, my cares all flown, a rich old man with a book of philosophy in his hand, nodding his age away. Ah, for such an ease what should a man not do ?

(*Exit* HENCHMAN.)

ACT IV.

SCENE.—MALONE'S *country house; a room.*

Enter HAROLD.

Yet does the logic of the eye outweigh
The logic of the mind—Is't possible?—
Is't not impossible?   Heaven and earth,
The vulture glutton feeds not on himself!
Yet often is the corporal sense awry.—
Nature doth not so rip herself apart
And cast her precious vitals to the dogs.—
Ha! there be more illusions in the mind
To make men fools than in the corporal sense.—
Her children's love, her honor, and her hope
Of Heaven—could she do't and forfeit these?
It stands not to reason.—Saw I not her—
Heard I not her voice, in love's position,
And the plaintive tone?   I think it cannot,
That it ought not be, but that I see I know.

Enter MALONE.

MALONE.

You desire to see me, Harold?

HAROLD.

Sir, I desire in that beggarly way

That words admit of, to apologize
For my unfilial conduct to you.   Oh!

MALONE.

Harold, even as you spoke I pardoned,
Knowing your acts were based on misconception·

HAROLD.

Fain would I plead exemption for those acts
Upon the basis of my ignorance;
But now my eyes are two full moons that glare
From heaven's heights upon the wanton earth.
A school-boy's piece!—O God, that I might speak,
Yet hear not my voice, know not its import.

MALONE.

Harold, you are sick.

HAROLD.

        Of a dread disease
That knows no remedy; playmate of death;
The skull and crossbone toy of this old world,
The sport of quacks and jest of medicine.
Where neath the sun grows that fair herb whose
    juice
Can salve a breach in honor, cure wounded love,
Or heal the rent that patent bastardy
Tears in a child's heart?

MALONE.

        You are overwrought
By study, Harold; I fear you have not slept.

HAROLD.

Slept! slept! why, sir, I saw a sight to-night
That cried aloud to all the sleeping tombs,
Awake! awake! the judgment is at hand,
The world is done, sleep no more forever!

MALONE.

This uncontrolled demeanor is foreign
To your ways.   Calm yourself, if you would speak.

HAROLD.

Why, I am as calm as a dead ocean.
Sir, I have something of great importance
To tell you, which, though it break your heart,
I pray you allow it not to disturb you.
Out on address! it is the bawd that comes
In the pale smock of an injured wife
And plants polluted kisses on a son.

MALONE.

You shoot me through the heart.

HAROLD.

                Sir, a problem
Or two in the ethics of human conduct.
If one should know a friend's wife had betrayed
Her husband, would it be a friendly act
To tell him of her infidelity?

MALONE.

The acme of disinterested friendship;
But, oh, I fear the question's import.

HAROLD.

One more: If a son should know his mother
Had to his father been untrue, how now
Would it be the part of filial duty
To keep the secret locked up in his breast,
Making his being putrid with its foulness?

MALONE.

I know too well the meaning of your words.
Your mother, Harold, my wife, your mother?

HAROLD.

By the infinity of chances, sir;
Excepting which I might have been an owl
And hooted at the moon, a weed or tree,
The deadly vapor of a tropic swamp,
An atom to float in nihilism—
The gaped at wonder of a race of fools.

MALONE.

No, no, no, Harold, be not light at this.

HAROLD.

Light? Oh, I am light! throw me overboard
And I will rise down a million fathoms.

MALONE.

What have you seen to throw you in this mood?

HAROLD.

Sir—for I dare not for the love of truth,
Address you as my father any more—
Have you observed in my mother's conduct

8

Any act smacking of impropriety
With your friend Maurice?

MALONE.

Oh, I have feared it!
Inscrutable Providence whose great design
Has thus to you unfolded that which I
Had with my cold lips sealed forever from you!—
Take warning bawds! though you be coy as snakes
And seek the covert of a cave, your deeds
Shall blaze like Ætnas to the gaping world.

HAROLD.

Have you known this thing and not redressed it?

MALONE.

Alas! I fear that you have seen much more
Than I have seen.

HAROLD.

I have seen, sir, and heard.

MALONE.

What, what?

HAROLD.

A woman with my mother's face
Slink, like a wanton, under night's cover
To meet her paramour.

MALONE.

What! no, Harold.

HAROLD.

Yes; and I heard her beg for her dishonor
As a sucking child cries for its mother's breast.

MALONE.

Where was that thunderbolt of Jove that strikes—

HAROLD.

And then he packed her off into a place
Wherein the modest stars might not behold
Her infidelity, and shaming cease to shine.

MALONE.

You are wrong, wrong; it has not gone so far.

HAROLD.

Have you known this thing and not redressed it?

MALONE.

I have but seen their winks, their knowing looks,
Their lover's nods and smiles.

HAROLD.

        Heaven and earth!

MALONE.

For nature could not these conditions hide;
Yet ever this poor merit has she had
That such a crime seemed quite impossible.

HAROLD.

It cannot be, is the fool's argument,
The dotard's recompense for lost love,
The cuckold's opiate, that to the quietude
Of self-deception, lulls us when we dare not look,
And know that what is is.   Out on such logic!

MALONE.

But to be certain of their crime and yet

Not have the proof of it is to be damned
Without redress.   O Harold, this it is
That to my patience gives the marks of sufferance.

HAROLD.

To have the rank stench in the nose and yet
Wait till the brain is poisoned unto death?

MALONE.

No, Harold, but to hold our patience reined
Until we have the proof of that degree
That not a loop is left for her escape.
In this be governed by my judgment, son.

HAROLD.

But she may catch the scent, and leave us held
Betwixt the certainty of guilt and lack
Of evidence—a life of hanging.

MALONE.

There's the redemption of pollution, that once
The film of chastity is pierced, no power
In Heaven or earth can e'er restore it.
Unchastity is a sore that never cures;
The proof we seek will come uncalled, yet come.

HAROLD.

Oh, that we centers of a lawgirt world
Alone should be transgressors of its laws !

(*Exit* HAROLD.)

MALONE.

At night, did he not say ?—in the park—
Clandestine meeting—begging dishonor !—

What means this? Oh, if she be false to me !—
What do I care ?—And yet, that is a lie
Told to me by myself,—for all the mines
In the rich earth I would not have her false—
With Bourne ?— the man I more than any hate—
I am half convinced of it. His eyes, hair his—
Oh, 'tis one thing to be false to one's wife,
And another thing to have one's wife false !
Though I hate her as I do sin, and she
Be ugly as an ape, dull as a worm,
And tasteless as a stone, yet if she be
False to me, she deserves a dozen deaths.
This fellow Henchman is a subtle dog.
He is under this, and would plot my wife
Into crime and laugh at my discomfort.
He shall explain this thing, and here he comes.

  Enter HENCHMAN.

Is my wife false to me ?

    HENCHMAN.

     S-s-s-h! certain, man,
Unless you have escaped the common rule.

    MALONE.

Are you a villain?

    HENCHMAN.

     If you think I am,
Then to you I am. If you think I am not,
Then to you I am not, for no one, sir,
Is a liar, nor a thief, nor a villain
Except as some one thinks him to be such.
The reason is plain; will you hear it?

MALONE.

Oh, you could *reason* a man into hell.

HENCHMAN.

Yes, most men, without trouble; but trust me,
I could never reason them out again.
But what ails your holiness?

MALONE.

Is my wife false?

HENCHMAN.

The very incarnation of falseness,
As you desired it.

MALONE.

You lie, you villain!

HENCHMAN.

First, you ask me if I am a villain,
Now you answer yes, and add me liar.
You hire me to prove the falseness of your wife,
When 'tis done you pay me off in curses.
You break my heart (*laughing*).

MALONE.

Ha!

HENCHMAN.

Hu!

MALONE.

Devil !

HENCHMAN.

Devilette!

MALONE.

Henchman!

HENCHMAN.

Malone!

MALONE.

Doctor, how came my wife—

HENCHMAN.

By the grace of God.

MALONE.

In the park at night—

HENCHMAN.

You are answered.

MALONE.

With this fellow Bourne?

HENCHMAN.

Oh, 'twas the foulest act in the whole play!

MALONE.

Explain this, sir.

HENCHMAN.

Thou me a little first.

MALONE.

O doctor, have we not been bosom friends?
Has not my purse been open as my heart?

HENCHMAN.

Oh! now you melt me down. Edmund, come
here—
In confidence?

MALONE.

Yes.

HENCHMAN.

Utter confidence?
And you will not allow your righteous wrath
To vent itself on me for telling truth?

MALONE.

Oh, never!

HENCHMAN.

Oh, beware of jealousy!
Edmund, has not your wife a handkerchief
Spotted with strawberries? (MALONE *going*).   This
    day did I
On such a one, see Maurice wipe his nose.

(*Exit* MALONE.)

Oh, you will try again to make an ass of me!
I am not so old but I know grain from chaff,
Yet whether he be honest in his villainy
Or hypocritical in his virtue
I am in doubt; for I have heard a lie
Oft told becomes the truth to him who tells it.

Enter CATHERINE.

Dear madam, if I may, I hope and trust
Your interview with Maurice in the park
Tended to your advantage.

CATHERINE.

As yet, sir,
I do not know, Maurice will do for me
What lies within his power.

HENCHMAN.

      Which God grant
May be much. When do you next see Maurice?

CATHERINE.

I know not,—when he shall see my husband.

HENCHMAN.

What, did you not arrange the time?

CATHERINE.

        No, sir.

HENCHMAN.

Nor the place either?

CATHERINE.

     I did not think of that.

HENCHMAN.

Tut, tut! my injunctions have gone for naught.

CATHERINE.

Alas! have I here made an error, sir?

HENCHMAN.

You should have set a time and place to get
His answer.

CATHERINE.

    Will you arrange it for me?

HENCHMAN.

With pleasure, madam; yet I think 'twere best—
I have a kind of foolish backwardness
In this affair, being but slightly known
To Maurice—if you would simply write a note

And let me take it to him, it would lend
A kind of zest or impulse to his act—
Make him dispatch it with more earnestness.

CATHERINE.

Why, so I will.

(*She sits to write.*)

HENCHMAN.

                    Slightly importune him,
As that the time drags until you see him.

CATHERINE.

Heaven knows it has a moping pace.
To-morrow night?

HENCHMAN.

          At the same hour and place.
And pray you, madam, pass a little further
To the rearward of the garden house—
The foliage there is denser.

CATHERINE.

                    Ah, doctor,
How kindly you have always treated me.

HENCHMAN.

Think not of me, dear lady; all my thoughts
And services, though by old age enfeebled,
Are as much at your command as though you were
My sovereign queen and I your humblest servant.

(*Exit* HENCHMAN.)

Enter HAROLD *unobserved by* CATHERINE.

CATHERINE.

O thou great Guardian of the world,
To me be merciful, forgive my sins
And to my mother's heart preserve my children's
    love.
Here in the just hands of Heaven I place my
    cause.

               (*Exit* CATHERINE.)

HAROLD.

She has named Heaven her judge—a just Court.
Shall I usurp the stern prerogative
Of nature?   Is not a violated law
Its own executor?   Infinite Judge,
Who can all mitigation see, shall I,
Who am into confusion thrown to view
A single point, and am but flesh and blood,
At most her equal—shall I turn judge,
And her presumptuously condemn to infamy?
May something not extenuate her guilt?
A husband's coldness, her children's absence,
The idleness of wealth, the heart's demands,—
When nature strays shall nature's man condemn?—
And, like a robber spotted in the act,
Shall I, unwarranted, immure her, nor
Let her these suspicious incidents explain?
Why, she is not unchaste,—'twould make an end
Of decency and murder modesty.
Now I will call her back, lay bare my thought;
Let her explain and set all things to right (*going*).
Nay, I'll not do't, 'twould be indelicate;

Why does she not herself make mention of it?
And yet I will recall her, and to her
So distantly and indirectly speak
That, being innocent, she shall not see
My purpose, and being putrid guilty,
Cannot conceal her guilt.   Mother, mother!
Now I am not prepared to question her.

Re-enter CATHERINE.

CATHERINE.

Harold, did you not call me?

HAROLD.

Yes, mother, yes.
(*Aside*) Heaven help me.—I know not how to
broach it.

CATHERINE.

Harold, what can your mother do for you?

HAROLD (*aside*).

Why now, hear that—sure she is innocent.—
Nothing, mother, nothing; I did not call.

CATHERINE.

You would speak, Harold, of your mother's grief.
I know the gentle spirit you conceal.

HAROLD (*aside*).

The very cunning of it.—O mother,
My heart is sore.

CATHERINE.

Nay, is it not enough
That I should grieve?   It will all come right.

HAROLD.

What think you, mother, of this thing called virtue?
Is it a substance; has it a being
In itself apart from all utility
Of time and place, surroundings and effects?
Or is it but a name, an airy ghost
Culled from the visionary brains of fools,
To fright the world from pleasure—how is this?

CATHERINE.

Why, Harold, you know your mother is not versed
In these great themes.

HAROLD.

       'Tis sure the chief sophism
Of a brainless world to claim that any act
Has virtue in itself?

CATHERINE.

       I know not that.

HAROLD.

But if the time and circumstance be pat,
Where lies the harm? 'Tis done; 'tis deaf; all's
    well.

CATHERINE.

Sure I am mazed to know your meaning, son.

HAROLD.

But is there not a universal law
Drawn from ten thousand years of life
That bids defiance to empiric fools?

CATHERINE.

Alas! your learning is beyond my grasp.

HAROLD.

Why look you here; is virtue not the essence
Of a woman?

CATHERINE.

It is her being's soul,
The thing without which she would forfeit Heaven.

HAROLD.

But custom, mother, custom, nothing else.
Had the world grown in loose licentiousness,
To be unchaste would be most virtuous.

CATHERINE.

Why, Harold, you affright me with such words.

HAROLD.

Nay, mother, I was pretending, only.
As the world waxed, unchastity has waned.
Time was when men and women roamed like
     beasts;
Came next the era when a humble man
Would with a score of women be content,
Or women with a dozen lovers; now—
Mark how we advance! one man, one woman,
Lovers none,—except it be the husband's friend.
Of late the world has grown so monstrous good
I hardly think there are above a score
Of women on the earth who are not pure.

CATHERINE.

I cannot see, my son, how there is one.

HAROLD.

And yet I once saw one, and mark you well
How outraged nature on her stamped his curse.
The blush of innocence was painted out;
The pretty eyes, which once for shyness
Dared not lift their lids, into a steely glare
Of brazen affrontery, were changed;
And lips, which might have borne the early imprint
Of a mother's kiss, had beastly commerce
Sapped of all their meaning when she grinned a
    smile;
And all her features so distorted were
As she had gone to hell to make her visage up.

CATHERINE.

Oh, horrible!

HAROLD.

               Yet see how chastity
Does finer than a spider's silver web
Upon a woman's visage draw his silken lines.

CATHERINE.

What think you, Harold, that you have spoken
    thus?

HAROLD.

I was thinking—I was thinking— thinking,
Of my—father. Good-night, mother, good-night.
I have some thoughts to think ere I retire.

(*He assists his mother hurriedly to the door.*)

(*Exit* CATHERINE.)

Enter HENCHMAN, *unobserved by* HAROLD.

Now either this be utter innocence
Or the very cunning of practiced guilt,
The which in action are twin born sisters.
Mark how she shook when I described the bawd!
Yet one not guilty might have done that too.
Why, look at her whole life of purity—
Shall it not overweigh this ounce of doubt?
It is a firmament of bright fixed stars,
Whose light shall this suspicious meteor
Extinguish never.   She is not guilty.

HENCHMAN (*aside*).

Wavering?   Then these be my arguments (*holding
up letters*).

(*As* HAROLD *sees* HENCHMAN *the latter
pretends to attempt to conceal the letters
in his pocket.*)

HAROLD.

Henchman, what have you there?

HENCHMAN.

I? Nothing, sir.

HAROLD.

Nothing, nothing?   Why, Henchman, should a
man
At the concealment of mere nothingness
Make efforts such as these?   You have something—

I feel it—about—oh, heavens !—about
That woman.   Give it me this instant.

HENCHMAN.

I have nothing that is to your concern.

HAROLD.

It is a lie; you have that there concerns me
In my birth, my life, my honor, my all.
I saw letters but a short moment since,
Which your attempt to hide convinces me
I have a right to see, and now produce them.

HENCHMAN.

Why, Heaven help me, are you void of shame?

HAROLD.

Deliver them, or I will take them from you.

HENCHMAN.

Are you my sovereign, I your subject bore,
That you do dare command me in this way?
Tut! if you think so, you had better have
At your address the means to execute
Your mandate, as you speak so like a king.

HAROLD.

See you these hands?   Think you that they would
    pause
At such a very pigmy as you are?

HENCHMAN.

Boy, I have the age to be your father—

HAROLD.

I care not if you are old as Adam.

HENCHMAN.

And though the white and black are mingled here—

HAROLD.

The letters.

HENCHMAN.

I have an oaken body—

HAROLD.

Dare you trifle?

HENCHMAN.

I dare defend my rights.

(*They struggle for the letters.*)

HAROLD.

It is my right.

HENCHMAN.

Shame, shame! respect my age.

Oh! oh! I am too old.

HAROLD (*taking the letter*).

Old man, forgive.

HENCHMAN.

You have o'ercome me and taken the notes.
I know not what they may contain, and 'twas
For your sake I refused you sight of them.
Now on your own head rest the consequence
Of this rash act.

Enter MALONE.

Oh! oh! I am near killed.

MALONE.

Why, what offense is here?

HAROLD (*reading the letter*).

Dear MAURICE: *The hours drag with a weary pace till I again shall see you. Meet me at the same time and place to-morrow night.*—CATHERINE.
I will be there.—MAURICE.

There's the offense, sir, if you have the nose.
Whence came these letters? Whence came these
    letters?

HENCHMAN.

One from your mother—

HAROLD.

              Hated appellate !

Use some other name.

HENCHMAN.

Your father's wife—

HAROLD.

Nor that either—oh, world of sin !—say she.

HENCHMAN (*picking up letters*).

Then she—pure woman !—who did write this one,
Begged me to give it to your father's friend,
And all unknowing that it held such vile
Proposals, I took it to the gentleman.
A certain mood with which he took and read it,
An amorous blush that overspread his face
As he perused and re-perused the letter,

Roused my suspicions, and when he noted not
I picked it up, intending to consign it
To the flames.   This is his answer; the two
Speak for themselves; you know as much as I.

(*Exit* HAROLD.)

Watch him close; for three nights he has not slept,
And untold dangers live in such a brain.

Re-enter HAROLD.

HAROLD.

There is no hell save earth, and devils none
But wear clothes.   Have you eyes that can behold
The beastly sight and not be blotted out?

MALONE.

We must prevent it.

HAROLD.

And live suspended

Betwixt the past crime and a future chance.
Let it go on—there's justice in our course—
We will be there and trip them ere the act.

(*Exeunt omnes.*)

ACT V.

MALONE'S *country place; a park with a flower-house; night.*

Enter a MAN *and a* WOMAN.

MAN.

It's curious how we were brought here from the city so suddenly.

WOMAN.

I'm half afraid. Do you know where we are?

MAN.

Since we left the station in the carriage I can't tell exactly, but I know about the place.

Enter HENCHMAN.

HENCHMAN.

What's that?—and what's that in me? To walk through the park—sure, 'tis nothing—but to walk with this thing by me! An infamous undertaking! I'll quit it here. Avaunt, you devil! They were to be here at this hour.

MAN.

Halloo!

HENCHMAN.

Are you the man and woman who were sent from the city to meet a man here?

MAN.

'Ve were sent here by some one that we didn't knów to meet a man.   Are you the man, and what do you want?

HENCHMAN.

I want you to help me play a joke, ha! ha! ha! —a devilish good joke!

MAN.

Well, for the best joke in the world we can't come here for nothing.

HENCHMAN.

Certainly not.   Here's a twenty for you each.

MAN.

That's good; now what's your joke?

WOMAN.

It must be awful funny for so much money.

HENCHMAN.

Ha! ha!--Well you see, my dear, I am one of those fellows who never cares for money when he can play a good joke.   I am here visiting a country friend of mine—a regular dolt--and I have sworn to him that this house is haunted.   (*Laughing.*)

MAN *and* WOMAN.

Haunted!

HENCHMAN.

Yes; has spirits, ghosts, in it, you know.

MAN.

Why, who the devil believes in ghosts?

WOMAN.

Well, I'm not so sure.

HENCHMAN.

Why, nobody believes in ghosts, of course. There's the joke of it, and that's why I have brought you here to play the joke. I've told my friend that I've seen the spirit of a man and woman in this house at night, and have laid him a bet that he can see them here to-night. Ha! ha!—you see?

MAN.

Ha! ha! We're to be the ghosts, ha! ha!

HENCHMAN.

Not so loud, you might raise the ghosts. Now I want you to put on these wigs and things (*the man and woman put on disguises, which make them resemble* BOURNE *and* CATHERINE) and then go into this house. By-and-by you will see a man and woman pass this way, and following them will be two men with me. When you see me lift my cane, so, you woman raise the window, put your head out and cautiously look around; then get back and put the window down. After that you sit in his lap—

WOMAN.

Is that the way ghosts do?

HENCHMAN.

That's the joke of it, for I've told this country lout that these ghosts act that way. When we look in at the window scream and run out the back way and make to the carriage quickly.

MAN.

Capital joke this.

HENCHMAN.

S-s-s-h! Go in now.

(*They go in and* HENCHMAN *locks the door.*)
The moon does muffle up her face to view
An act so vile. Ha, 'tis a mucky deed!—
If I were out of it the wealth of earth
Could not again entice me into it.

(*Exit* HENCHMAN.)
Enter BOURNE *and* CATHERINE, *followed at a distance by* MALONE, HAROLD *and* HENCHMAN. BOURNE *and* CATHERINE *pass around the flower-house by the door, which is so arranged that* HAROLD *cannot see it.* HENCHMAN *lifts his cane and the* WOMAN *raises the window and follows* HENCHMAN's *previous instructions.*

HENCHMAN.

Who would have thought her to have been so wise?

MALONE.

That argues great experience.

HAROLD.

Oh, vile act !

Can they live ? Shall they live ? Shall they not
die ?

MALONE.

O Harold, let her conscience be her hangman.
Death would to her be sweeter than remorse.

(*They look in at the window; then* HAR-
OLD *suddenly tries the door; screams in-
side and exeunt* MAN *and* WOMAN;
HENCHMAN *grapples with* HAROLD.)

HENCHMAN.

Boy, boy, beware of rashness !

HAROLD.

Let me go.

HENCHMAN.

Help me, Malone !

HAROLD.

Unloose me, sir ; away!

MALONE.

Have mercy on her.

HAROLD.

Justice demands death.

MALONE.

She is your mother.

HAROLD.

'Tis a beastly lie,—

She is a harlot, and has lived too long.

Oh, if you loose me not—

MALONE.

Harold!   Harold!

HAROLD.

Not though your arms were chains.   Are you a
    man—

Oh, shame, shame!   Where is your honor that you
    can

On this act look and let the guilty live?

Go boast of your dishonor,—away from me!

(Breaks from them and exit.)

MALONE.

He will kill them.

HENCHMAN.

These are well on their way.

If he escape the others 'tis a fortune.

See! they come, drawn hither by the noise.

The time is yours; now summon all your strength;

Lay every nerve and muscle to your will.

Wear you a face of thunder; look fierce as hell,

And when you strike leave terror in your wake!

So drive them hence, as out of Eden

Jehovah drove the first great sinners.

(Exit HENCHMAN.*)*

Enter CATHERINE *and* BOURNE, *running.*

CATHERINE.

Where was it?

BOURNE.

Sure, near here.

CATHERINE.

'Twas Harold's voice.
He cried *unloose me*, as though robbers had him.
My husband!

MALONE.

How now, woman! throbs your heart?
O Kate, that I should find you in this act!

CATHERINE.

Alas! what act?

MALONE.

That vice should in such shape
Enrobe itself!

BOURNE.

Edmund, in Heaven's name—

MALONE.

Oh, in the name of hell, rather say you!
Destroyer of my peace, my happiness,
My home; betrayer of my wife; traitor
To holy friendship's cause—you who for years
Have lived upon my honor and my life—

CATHERINE.

Edmund, what mean you?—I am stricken dumb.

MALONE.

'Tis time, 'tis time. O wretch unnamable!

BOURNE.

Sure you are mad, for this cannot be sport.

MALONE.

The very cunning of a mind diseased—
I am that fool who comes to beg of you
The honor of my wife.   I am grown old
And my children need it.   Can you not patch
The rent made in a woman's virtue, piece up
The broken fragments of a wife's honor,
And to the husband make the scar unseen?
Where is the honor of my wife?

CATHERINE.

O Edmund!

BOURNE.

Thought I you sane, those words should be your
    last.

MALONE.

The very thing : steal first the honor of the wife
Then seek a pretext for the husband's murder.
Here is my heart, come both of you and take
The flesh, since you have stolen its immortal part.
Oh, wring your hands as you have wrung my heart.

BOURNE.

Mean you, Malone, I have betrayed your wife?

MALONE.

Witness the deliberate villainy!
The very hardened iciness of crime.
Or do you mean to play upon the words?

'Tis no matter if you say betrayed,
Stolen, robbed, plundered or purchased,
Honor, virtue, chastity or what not;
You have taken that which was neither mine
Nor hers, nor any one's to give, but was
A gift from Heaven, a loan at birth——
To be returned at death—that without which
A woman is a mass of rotten flesh——
That you have stolen and left her what you see.

BOURNE.

Down on your knees; for this gross insult beg
The pardon of your wife, or else I kill you.

CATHERINE.

Hold! stay! Maurice, he is still my husband.

BOURNE.

Am I a man, to see you so outraged?

CATHERINE.

Mine honor's purity is not thus soiled.
My fate is yonder and I fear him not.

MALONE.

Out of my sight—you public shames, away!

BOURNE.

Ha! public shames!

CATHERINE.

Peace, Maurice, peace,—
A word and I am gone—'tis wondrous
What a mighty calmness steals upon me.
Edmund, I have endured your insults,

Stood your taunts, by your disdain been withered,
Crouched 'neath your formless charges and begged
    you
Give them shape.—This, and more than tongue
    can tell,
I have borne from you, hoping to win you back,
And I as innocent of any crime
As is the newest babe.   It was the wife—
The loving and obedient wife—
Such as my mother taught me how to be,
That bid me do all this.   But now you have
Impeached my chastity, and this shaft pierces
Beyond the wife and strikes the woman,
And 'gainst this last and heinous outrage
Every atom of the woman in me
Stands up in fierce rebellion.—Oh, witness thou
Who art beyond the stars, how innocent I am !—
Enough.   I leave you now as spotless
As that day you took me as your wife,
But going shall demand, if there be justice,
In this world the rights which God has given me.
           (*Exeunt* CATHERINE *and* BOURNE.)

Re-enter HENCHMAN.

HENCHMAN.

To dare to do the deed is one thing.   Aye,
But to carve the bird through the joints—'tis that,
In faith, which tries the skilled anatomist.
The devil bows and bids your holiness godspeed.

MALONE.

Out. you dog !

HENCHMAN.

Dare you say so much?

MALONE.

Be gone!

HENCHMAN.

Ha! ere the sun has tipped yon peaks with gold
The wired spark shall to the globe's end have
    flashed
Your infamy.

MALONE.

Stay! forgive me, Doctor.

HENCHMAN.

Forgive, the devil!

MALONE.

But I meant it not.

HENCHMAN.

Before you sleep to-night, put in this hand
A hundred thousand dollar check on bank,
Or, by my soul, I send you to perdition.

MALONE.

So much?

HENCHMAN.

Not a farthing less. ·

MALONE.

Ah! I see.

You are in some emergency for means.
The check is yours. When one friend does re-
    fuse

Another help, how meanly looks the act.

HENCHMAN.

Indeed it does; and I have late observed
How bad the old world is become, till now
Virtue has laid aside her past white robe
And wears the raiment of necessity,—
Foul, tarnished garment, it makes the nose ill.

MALONE.

Indeed, I greatly fear it is the case.

(*Exit* MALONE.)

HENCHMAN.

How unexpected fortune falls upon us!
That his rash words have given me the chance
To say the words at which I long have paused.
This money in my hand, the devil take his cause.

(*Exit* HENCHMAN.)

Re-enter CATHERINE *and* BOURNE.

BOURNE.

No more, Catherine, no more.

CATHERINE.

I cannot go.
It was the injured woman then that spoke;
I am the wife and loving mother now.
Maurice, will my children think my virtue gone?
Heavenly powers, let them not think so!
Madness is in that thought—I will go wild.
I must look on my children ere I go;
From their sweet lips the dear assurance have

That they believe me pure.   God in Heaven,
Thou wilt not let me die and have them think
I am unchaste?   O Father, let me live
Till by some light from Heaven I prove
How innocent I am.

BOURNE.

Calmed be your mind—

CATHERINE.

They cannot think it, Maurice?

BOURNE.

No, no, no;
You are their idol; your children worship you,
And Nature's hand to your safe rescue coming,
Will teach their love their mother's purity.

CATHERINE.

O thank you, Maurice,—kind Heaven grant it.
Alas! to be discarded thus—turned out
To go alone, or go along with him
Who is with me accused of this foul crime,
And make suspicion sure,—flee like a thief
I know not where, in the dark, from my home;
What crime is done that on me innocent
This heavy visitation falls?   Ah, me!

BOURNE.

Our innocence must be the armor of our course.

CATHERINE.

Our trust in Heaven.   Fare thee well, Maurice,
Till I see my children.   Alas! that I
Should like a traitor slink into my home
And steal the kiss that should of right be mine.

(*Exit* CATHERINE.)

10

BOURNE.

If it be true there is an unseen hand
That guides the destiny of man, how stranger
Than the world itself its movements are.
'Tis these that make me doubt; these snap the cord
Of faith, making the universe an anarchy.
O Justice, hast thou no part in Divinity?

(*Exit* BOURNE.)

Re-enter HAROLD *followed by* CATHERINE.

CATHERINE (*aside*).

I saw him come this way; yes, 'tis Harold

HAROLD (*soliloquizing*).

My mother?—no, not she, yes, even she—
Even she whose labors gave to me birth—
O God! O God! become a harlot!
Even she who suckled me at her breast—
O murdered virtue! how could any one
Who from her body has sustained a life,
Make of that body uses such as these?
And after five and twenty years to turn—
Stopped be my breath that I speak not the word.
"Tis a curse—a curse of hell upon me
That my poor heart can bear this and not burst.—
When from her body the lascivious
Had been robbed by age to turn a lewd!
When at her feet the world's wealth lay, and she
Stripped of the shabby raiment of necessity
That e'en the veriest bawd can blazon
To the world as an excuse.—What is it?

A moment plunge from purity to this
After an age of virtue?—A fool's thought!
'Tis the remembrance of a hot young love—
This monster serpent was not born to-day.
It has—it has—it has lived before!
And I—I—who am I?   Who is my father?
My face, these eyes, this nose, this mouth, these
    cheeks,
And every lineament proclaims me bastard!

CATHERINE.

Harold!

HAROLD.

    Heavenly love, are your prayers said?
Where is your lover?

CATHERINE.

    I have no lover, Harold.

HAROLD.

Do you see yon hag?   She was sent down there
For lying.   There's another; mark how she
    writhes!
She sold her body as a passion slave,
And damned her soul.   Yes, but see yonder
    wretch;
She tore the family altar up
And used its cloth to light the fire of lust,
Made bastards of her children, her husband
Drove to the grave, and flung her offspring out
To the ravishment of wolves.

CATHERINE.

O Harold,
I am not guilty!

HAROLD.

What hellish power
Supports you in those words, when one short
    moment hence
You shall behold the yawning depths of hell?
Think it! one minute more and you shall stand—
Your sins labeled upon your naked soul—
Before that Judge who never errs.   Can you
Then say, *I have committed no adultery?*

CATHERINE.

My soul has not that sin which makes me fear
To meet my God—I am so innocent.

HAROLD.

O monstrous sin that can so stand undaunted
In the face of Heaven!   Yet I'll not do't—
Each rivulet that stained these hands would grow
A bloody river on my soul, or rise
Each one a snake, to fright me into hell
For safety's sake—O coward that I am!

CATHERINE.

You do not believe me guilty.   Say it,
O my son!

HAROLD.

Son, son!   True you did bear me,
But can you name my father?   Oh, cringing
    shame!
Remorse, if thou canst eat into a mother's heart,
Here is thy food.

CATHERINE.

Oh !

HAROLD.

    Who is my father ?
Or, if you know not, say it, and I'll go
Find him by his looks in the public ways.

CATHERINE.

Oh, do not kill me with these dagger words !

HAROLD.

Avaunt, you thing ! your manner owns your guilt.

CATHERINE.

If there be any dot upon my life—

HAROLD.

"Tis well if it be less than ulcer all.

CATHERINE.

O Harold, can you think that this poor frame—

HAROLD.

This sacred tenement of flesh.

CATHERINE.

     Oh, me !

HAROLD.

I will hear your reason.

CATHERINE.

     This poor body
That gave you birth, that fed your life,
And watched you grow from tiniest babyhood,
That for so many years followed your father

Through sickness and through poverty, could now
Commit so great a crime against her God,
Her children, husband, and against herself?

HAROLD.

Who could do acts like these, could say this, too,
And it affects me not.   I do not think I know.

CATHERINE.

Harold, I could have stood your father's taunts,
His hatred, his disdain, his accusations;
I could have borne the flings the world might cast
Upon me, the smarting slaps from papers,
The cruel gossip, the lies and calumnies;
But to have you, my son, whose words come only
From the deep convictions of your honest heart,
Accuse me, your mother, who so loves you
That she would give her life for yours, of lack
Of chastity—O God, what have I done
To cause this forfeit of my children's love?

HAROLD.

You can make me weep—my eyes are used to
    tears.

CATHERINE.

O Harold, throw aside these shady doubts,
And clearly peer into my life and heart.
Come to me, Harold; look into my face.
Do you see shame or guilt there?   Do these lips
Speak to you lies?   Do these eyes look to you
    lies?
Do I so act as one whose chastity is gone?

HAROLD.

If I had not seen it——

CATHERINE.

             Nay, but seen what?
If there be any speck upon my life——

HAROLD.

Why, what a slave am I!—eyes damning eyes,
Judgment with sense at war, reason and love
Contesting——the dust of every passion's wind.
Here is my only footing: I have seen
Your guilt, yet spared your life——leave me forever.

      Enter RICHARD *and* HELEN.

CATHERINE

O cruel, cruel son! cannot these tears
Plead with you, Harold?   Let me upon my knees
Before you, as you a little child were wont
To come to me with all your little woes,
And beg you do not think me gone to shame.

HAROLD.

O God! away! your presence makes me think
Of naught but death, damnation, hell——away!

HELEN.

Oh, what is this?

RICHARD.

         Harold, are you gone mad,
That you thus dare insult my mother?

HAROLD.

Cease, boy, you know not what you prate on.

RICHARD.

Where is that filial love that often you
Have chidden me with lack of?

HAROLD.

Dare you question?

HELEN.

For shame, Harold, for shame to act so!

HAROLD.

You too? well, well, go follow in her track.

RICHARD.

Beware, Harold! this lady is my mother.

CATHERINE.

Richard! Harold!

HAROLD.

Go keep her company.

HELEN.

Fear you not God's vengeance to dishonor thus
Your mother?

HAROLD.

She is herself dishonored.

RICHARD.

Retract that!

HAROLD.

Why, you puny imp, begone!

RICHARD.

Harold, I brand you the paid defamer
Of your own mother for your father's gold.

HAROLD.

Ha ! boy, I will tear you into pieces.

RICHARD.

If you can.

CATHERINE.

Hold, my sons (*goes between them*).

HAROLD.

Accursed name!

Come on, Richard.

CATHERINE.

You shall not fight.

RICHARD.

Come on.

HAROLD.

I have a dagger that was meant for me—

RICHARD.

I fear you not.

CATHERINE.

I am your mother, both,
And by that right command you to desist.

HAROLD (*bewildered*).

Richard—my father's gold—did you not say
My father's gold bribed me ?   I was dreaming.
Father ! father !—there they are—Oh, shame,
    shame !
Let it go on—I will be there with you.

(*Exit* HAROLD.)

Re-enter MALONE *on one side,* BOURNE *on
the other.*

MALONE.

Are you still here?   Hell fattens on your stay—
Get you gone, ere you have done a murder.

CATHERINE.

I am going now.

RICHARD.

Going, mother? where?

CATHERINE.

I do not know—your father drives me out.

RICHARD.

Why, then, he drives me out.

HELEN.

And Helen, too.

Re-enter HAROLD.

HAROLD.

Go get you to your beds—the night needs rest,
The world is cracked and nature is at war.
Come, ruin's dogs, and feast on this discord.
The world's a graveyard; life's but a nightmare,
And hell awaits us all—go to your posts.

(*Exeunt* HAROLD *and* MALONE *one side, the
rest on the other.*)

[In an age in which the patrons of the drama demand that their feelings be not too rudely shaken up, I am compelled to offer some sort of an apology for the introduction of a scene so wild as this. My purpose, of course, is to forcibly illustrate the breaking up of the family state, a civil war in the sovereignty of home. Those who can view this through the eyes of the chief character, and see in it something akin to the cracking up of a world, may appreciate my motive though they condemn the execution.—THE AUTHOR.]

ACT VI.

SCENE.—MALONE'S *house in San Francisco; a room.*

Enter HAROLD *and* HENCHMAN *opposite.*

HENCHMAN.

O Harold, you are looking very ill;
I fear me you are not so well to-day.

HAROLD.

Indeed !   Now what traitors our feelings are;
And how warped our judgment on our own looks.
I am that silly fool who courts himself
For a beauty.   Oh, I am grown the slave
Of the mirror, and come to think myself
The first of charmers.

HENCHMAN.

                I am glad to see
How light your spirits are.

HAROLD.

                Oh, heavens, yes!
My spirits have that leaden buoyancy—

And yet they have a most uncertain quality;
That sometimes when I laugh I weep—as 'twere
They slip the knot and fall a thousand miles
Into the ocean of my soul.

HENCHMAN.

For this
You must take something.

HAROLD.

Indeed, I must, sir;
Yet I know not what it should be, unless
It be my life.

HENCHMAN.

Tut, tut! some medicine.

HAROLD.

Sir, a little sport in the way of a conundrum:
Can you tell me the greatest trade in the world?

HENCHMAN.

I have not thought.

HAROLD.

Why, 'tis that of giving medicine.

HENCHMAN.

The proof?

HAROLD.

Its deeds.

HENCHMAN.

How so?

HAROLD.

Why, you have outwitted the Almighty, and
nature has succumbed before your efforts. Once
men had sound minds in healthy bodies, and died,
like other beasts, of old age. Now note the end
of your herculean task: a sound mind, a healthy
body, or a death by old age, is a museum wonder.

HENCHMAN.

I think you lay too much to bad doctoring.

HAROLD.

Very well, very well, father it where you will,
it's all one to mankind. There's not one of God's
human creatures in a thousand but is deformed,
crippled, or illshapen.

HENCHMAN.

You are too sweeping.

HAROLD.

Not a whit. Take the face: the eyes—bleared,
bold, squint, meaningless, villainous, shrewd, thriv-
ing—a hundred such to one that's fit to look on;
the nose—stub, hook, or crook, an outrage on
the face; the mouth—flabby, open, gaping,
loose, lascivious, long-lipped, short-lipped, grinning,
or villainously taut; the head malformed and ugly
generally.

HENCHMAN.

Hold!

HAROLD.

Yourself. Look at the rest of your man! The body—fat, blubbery, or lean and cadaverous; dwarfs and giants; hunchbacks and swaybacks and deformities *ad infinitum*. Oh, when you see one man or woman perfect formed, behold a million malformed, illshapen eyesores! And where's your being but has some pain—a weak stomach, bad liver, disordered kidneys, aching bones, decayed lungs, affected hearing, fading sight? Lord, what a thing has man degenerated into—a sickly, illshapen man of dirt. Out on it! the world had best begin again!

HENCHMAN.

But, Harold, you look at the outer man only— his mechanism merely. Behold the inner man, the mighty mind, the pure heart, the contrite—

HAROLD.

Sightless old idiot! Your inner man—your mental, moral, spiritual man! Why, this thing that covers us is a perfect paragon of beauty by the side of the hideous devil that lurks inside. Out on your inner man! He is a very mass of fallacy, corruption, dishonesty, and hypocrisy. His judgment—the spoiled instinct of the brute; his will—an arbitrary despot; his love—the coacher of his lust; his hate—the dictator of his interest; feelings, desires all, but purveyors to his appetites. Oh, your inner man is the most monstrous criminal

in the world—a committor of all the crimes on
the statute every day, a murderer when ruffled;
an adulterer at sight of a woman; a grasping
thief each minute; a secret blasphemer; a notorious
liar, lying even to himself; and as for that other
class of crimes called moral errors—hypocrisy, in-
sinuation, and their thousand sisters and brothers
—why, God save me! your inner man lives on them.
Oh, your inner man is a fine villain, a sharp,
shrewd villain, a villain who commits most of his
murders, adulteries, and other crimes, in thought;
for, mark you, his outer accomplice is as big a
coward as your inner man is a villain! What a
splendid thing, indeed, is your man, your inner
and outer deformity and outrage on nature!

HENCHMAN.

You look too much on the dark side of life.

HAROLD.

Life! what is life! The millionth hap of chance;
The breathing stone; the cackle of a clod; ·
Earth lust endowed; a feeling energy
To sport a moment in the wind of time
And then go back to nothing! Oh, woeful day
That nature capped her work and stung
Into unfeeling earth the power to suffer!

HENCHMAN.

You see it through the dark glass of your own eye.

HAROLD.

Are you here? Oh, very well, very well,
I would be alone; my mood is inward.

(*Exit* HENCHMAN.)

And this is life,—the thing for which we're born,—
The output of divinity?   Why, no—
Why, surely no—a fallacy of fools!
Yet in a drop of life what pleasures thrive;
To quaff the possibilities of which
Outweighs the ending of its pains.   'Tis this—
For this—we make our minds and bodies slaves,
That lends tenacity to earthly stay,
And cries a halt to e'en the crippled, blind,
Despised misery and cracked old age.
But what have I—besmerched by infamy,
All purpose dead and hope beyond a hope,
To hold me to a life that I despise?
The fear of death? a groundless apprehension!
Death is the well man's terror, nothing more (*takes
        a dagger in his hand*).
'Tis said, 'tis done, 'tis over, and oblivion
Like a shroud falls on existence—Charlotte!

  Enter Charlotte.

   CHARLOTTE.

Harold, are you alone?

   HAROLD.

    Alone, alone,—
Even to the exclusion of myself.

   CHARLOTTE.

No, Harold, not so lonely; there is one
Whose love, though it be sister's love, has yet
That constant quality it rivals life.

HAROLD.

Oh, you avenging powers which sometimes burst
Your wrath upon the wicked in their deeds,—
If ever scornful finger point at this pure head,
If ever viper whisper in her ear,
If ever eye unchastely look at her,
You forked fiery messenger of God,
Burn up the body ere the act is done,
And to perdition send his cursed soul !

CHARLOTTE.

O Harold !

HAROLD.

If you are honest, fear not.

CHARLOTTE.

You would not think me otherwise than pure ?

HAROLD.

No ; for the world I would not think so.
O you minx, you can hug, kiss, and betray
A man all in a minute.

CHARLOTTE.

My brother !

HAROLD.

'Tis so ; for once—O Heaven, a hundred times!—
My mother came to me, her eyes o'erbrimmed
With tears so sacred—yes, she—O God!—even
    she—
Her visage primed so full of innocence
It had drawn pity from a stone; and then--

11

Even then—when on her knees she prayed Heaven
To guard her from pretended wrong—O shame!
Her inner eye was searching for a place,
Her mind, that prayed, was planning out a way,
To play her husband false.

CHARLOTTE.

> Would I were dead—

HAROLD.

It kills my tongue to tell you, as it does
Your ear to hear this.   Leave me now, Charlotte.
Companionship with me has something deadly
In it, that smothers up the love of life.
I know the heart that throbs within your breast;
It is my own; I can feel it in you
Tugging and straining and trying to burst
The solid flesh that holds it prisoner.

(*Exit* CHARLOTTE.)

There's sure a god in life that guides our acts,
And stayed my hand which but a moment since
Had hurried off my life and unprotected left
My sister in the world.   Oh, 'tis the curse
Of fools, this thinking too much on themselves!

Enter HORTENS TECHNOR.

HORTENS.

This is Harold, son of Edmund Malone?

HAROLD.

Indeed!   Is it?   Ah, madam, you little know
Of what surpassing wisdom you are possessed.
Who are you?

HORTENS.

One, sir, who knows your father.

HAROLD.

Wise, very wise, mysteriously wise!
I would change places with you, when I think
You would be less informed than you are now.

HORTENS.

I have some knowledge of your parents' troubles.

HAROLD.

Ah! think not that you surprise me, madam;
Being a modest looker-on in the world,
I have observed this characteristic
Of your sex: that you take on the knowledge
Of others' troubles as though the bearing
Of the knowledge helped to bear the troubles.

HORTENS.

Peace, sir!   Though in my manner there may lurk
Suspicion—

HAROLD.

Pardon, madam, in your air
There is a certain and majestic grace
That makes. me think that you are carved from
      stone—
Or should be—or should be—for flesh is weak.

HORTENS.

I have come here as your friend—

HAROLD.

Ah, indeed!
Good, friendly madam, friends are like gnats;

In our summer time they swarm about us,
But in our winter era, I am told,
These insects do prefer the foulest dirt
To our poor company.   Yes, good madam,
Friends are as abundant in this great world
As other creeping things, and yet you might,
With the finest comb, scrape the universe
And ne'er catch one.   Does not the homeliness
Of my figures make you in love with them?

HORTENS.

There is a kinship in our feelings there
Which somewhat robs the language of its sting.
I am here to help you and am not deterred.

HAROLD.

Really, your kindness is excessive;
One of a mean and gross, suspicious turn,
Which, Heaven helping, nature gave me not—
Oh, I am soft as water, pliable
As dough, but point your finger at my head
And I will think your thoughts; yet, as I say,
One tinctured with suspicion might have thought
You had another object in this visit.

HORTENS.

I have seen the day those words had cost you;
But now I am so humbled in mine own
Esteem, I have no motive in my thoughts
Except to prove myself an honest woman.

HAROLD.

An honest woman?   Now Heaven preserve you!

How desolate and lonesome this world must seem.
Die, lady, die, and I will have erected
To your memory a monster monument
In the most public place on this broad earth.
A stately, solid column it shall be,
O'er-topping all the petty works conceived—
So tall that it shall do obeisance
To the sun as o'er the earth his daily
Concourse sweeps, and call the world to notice.
You on the top, worked by the finest sculptor
Of the age, shall stand, scorning the lustful earth,
And converse holding none save with the stars.
And yet you shall be made of hardest stone,
Lest e'er immortalized you fall; for once—
I knew a woman once, who fell when she
Had all the props of earth to hold her up—
O woman, if that cold face belie you not,
If you were but above the bribing power
Of wealth, by beauty unseducible,
Unswerved by lust, by honor only moved,
I would translate you to the clouds and cry
To all the world, *Behold, a woman has been born!*
Nay, note me not,—I am that rumbling fool
Who follows o'er the marshy earth a spark,
A fleeting nothing, that lives but in my brain,
Till sickened nature calls me to a stop,
And cries, *Thou fool!* Who are you, madam?
    speak.
· What want you? I have other things to do.

HORTENS.

You do my sex injustice.

HAROLD.

Well, well, well.

HORTENS.

I am not the being you suppose me,
Nor ye so bad as you might think me.

HAROLD.

To your theme.

HORTENS.

My name is Hortens Technor.

HAROLD.

You should have been a Greek, and made of stone.

HORTENS.

I am here to save your mother.

HAROLD.

Madam,
You should go save the heathen.

HORTENS.

To save her
From an outrage cowardly and infamous.

HAROLD.

A very cunning and well-spoken lie.

HORTENS.

May I speak?

HAROLD.

If you tell no lies.   Go on ;
Though, pardon madam, my ears are crammed
With such discord they may not hear you well.

HORTENS.

I, too, have had my wrongs.   These I might store
Down in my soul's deep solitude to sleep;
But on my wrongs another woman's rights
Repose; and here I swear, in telling this,
My solitary motive is to lift
From your unspotted mother that dark cloud
With which two scoundrels have enveloped her.

HAROLD.

An object laudable and plausible,
Yet methinks it sounds too well committed.

HORTENS.

May I speak?

HAROLD.

Conditioned as before.

HORTENS.

On the occasion of your father's visit
To this city, when first his golden wealth
Revealed him to the wondering world, I met him;
He loved me from the first.

HAROLD.

If that be false,
It has the merit of some interest.

HORTENS.

His honest way of wooing caused no thought
That he was other than a single man.
His hotly pressed affection by degrees
Grew on me till at length I loved him
With all the ardor of a nature deep,
If not impulsive.

HAROLD.

     I cry you pause!—
The unknown quantity in wedded life,
The x in the equation of our married state.—
Ha! you mistress—

HORTENS.

    By heavens you wrong me !

HAROLD.

Go, get you to your brothel—

HORTENS.

     You wrong me—
I am not wicked, as my acts will show.

HAROLD.

Then get to Heaven, or you will soon be.

HORTENS.

Alas! you are mad to talk so.

HAROLD.

       Alas !
Are there no fathers left to prey upon,
No families whole to break and quarter?

HORTENS.

I knew not he was married till too late.

HAROLD.

There's some redemption for you in that fact—
Why, who am I, that have a mother like you,
That I dare rail so loud at your disgrace ?

HORTENS.

I say you wrong me there; I loved him
With the warranty of love, not lust.

HAROLD.

I have it so; you loved him; he loved you;
You knew not he was married—the tale drags.

HORTENS.

Then burst the meteor of his marriage
On my cloudless sky—

HAROLD.

               I am not critical.

HORTENS.

Post haste I charged him with his infamy,
But his protesting love and cunning lie,
Drove off determination from her throne
And sat a foul usurper there.   He said—
Meanwhile heaving a thousand broken sighs—
That his wife had broken her marriage vows,
And that he was about to institute
Proceedings for divorce; that for my love
He wished it ended before I knew it,
And when 'twas over we should be united.
I listened, doubted, but love o'ercame me,
And I believed him.

HAROLD.

        And like the fable
Of the cat and monkey—

HORTENS.

O, hear me, sir!
"Twas but a night ago he came to me
Deep flushed with wine, and either from that cause,
Or from that other one which makes a man
Tell to a woman things which he would not
To his own mind confess, with raillery
He told me that a certain Doctor Henchman,
Yourself, and he, had seen the faithlessness
Of your mother, and the divorce would soon
Be granted.

HAROLD.

On, on, on—stop not on that!

HORTENS.

The boldness of the act and its relator
Abashed me, and led me on to discourse
On the depravity of such a thing;
Saying, above all things it passed wonder
How any woman could to him be faithless.
This seemed to touch him in a tender point,
For straight a solemn aspect overcame
His raillery; then he paused; then wavered;
And then, with a shrewd cunning in his eye,
He winked, and said he would confess to me—
To only me, for that in me he had
Such confidence he knew I would not tell it,
That it was naught but talk and balderdash
About his wife's unfaithfulness to him.

HAROLD.

Oh, if I have wronged her, may Providence
Put out these eyes to never see her more!—
Woman, let what you speak be true or die.

HORTENS.

So is it word for word. And more, he said
That the appearance of your mother's guilt
Had been produced by this man Henchman,
To furnish evidence for the divorce.

HAROLD.

This is a lie; I saw it all myself.

HORTENS.

Nay, hold, and I will tell you of that, too.
At such tremendous infamy I grew
Indignant, and formed the resolution
There and then to save your mother from it;
To which end I gave him good encouragement
To tell me all, with a pleased mien my purpose
Well concealing. Then he related to me
The dreadful story of that awful night
When he led you, his son—O sovereign shame!—
To look into the window of some house
There to behold your mother and the man.

HAROLD.

O kill, do not refresh my memory!

HORTENS.

Wait, sir,—'twas not your mother that you saw,
Nor Bourne, but two masked bawds by Hench-
     man's hand
Cunningly disposed there to deceive you.

HAROLD.

Go on, liar; tell me I am not here;
Tell me the world is not; dispute my being;
Show that the sun is but a red-hot pot,
By the blowing of the cook's breath kept so.
I am a little baby, to be told
Of giants, goblins, fairies, devils, gods.—
Come, be my nurse, fair lady, sing a song.

HORTENS.

And unto this my fair intentions come.

HAROLD.

Oh, now, if she be pure —

HORTENS.

           And she is pure.

HAROLD.

What depth of hell can my accursed soul
Find fit for punishment?—Dare I again
Behold her, see her piteous face?—
Oh, hers were tears which might have melted stone,
Moved trees to weep, or anything save me!

HORTENS.

She will forgive you.

HAROLD.

           Oh, never, never!

HORTENS.

I know she will—

HAROLD.

You know she will?—Why, then,
You come from her to work my feelings up.

HORTENS.

I never saw her.

HAROLD.

Away, away!
This is another scheme to murder truth.—
I have too long been but the sport of plots,
And whipped about by every wind that blows.

HORTENS.

O sir, if there be any test of honesty
Put me to it, and if I fail, then rest
Upon me everlasting infamy.

HAROLD.

Will you face my father and say these things?

HORTENS.

I will face him, or any man, or place.

HAROLD.

Then I will do't.—These things can be no worse
Than they are now. Madam, take yonder room;
Anon I will explain my purpose to you.
                              (*Exit* HORTENS.)
Now will I send for them and fetch them all
So facing one another as shall try
Their several honesty of purpose.
                              (*Exit* HAROLD.)

Enter HENCHMAN *with a pocket book.*

Who would not rather have a hundred thousand dollars in his pocket, than twice that sum and have his body locked in jail?

Ah! my little bank notes, how are you?

Henchman, come into Court!—Henchman away in Germany among the mysteries. Henchman, come into Court!—Henchman smiling at the sphynx. Henchman, come into Court!—Henchman snoozing in the land of Budda.

Ah! my wiley lawyer, fare you well,
My carpet bag is packed and I'm off to—Germany.

Enter GLASCO.

GLASCO.

Is Malone in?

HENCHMAN.

In where?

GLASCO.

Is Malone at home?

HENCHMAN.

That depends on the meaning of the word *home.*

GLASCO.

Is Malone here?

HENCHMAN.

Go ask his valet; if he knows not, try his harlot.

Enter MALONE.

MALONE.

Sir, I would I had a better heart to bid you welcome.

HENCHMAN (*his handkerchief to his eyes*).

Sir, I would I had a better heart to bid you—
farewell.

GLASCO.

Your wife has answered your petition for divorce,
and I have called to talk with you concerning it.

MALONE.

It was very kind of you to come here.

(*Exeunt* MALONE *and* GLASCO.)

HENCHMAN.

Oh! he will charge you for it, never fear.

(*Exit* HENCHMAN.)

Re-enter HAROLD *and* HORTENS.

HORTENS.

Will you not say what you expect of me?

HAROLD.

I have not dared allow my expectation bloom,
But have nipped off each tender shooting bud
And planted it all in soil most sterile.
But should I tell you that of everything
Which I would have you do, it would be this:
Prove, O prove my mother that pure angel
I was wont to think her ere damnation came.

HORTENS.

To do this is the end and not the means.
I thought you had laid out a course for me.

HAROLD.

You are the actress, woman,—not I;
And howsoever good my plan might be,
If you fail in the acting it is naught.
I have provided here a little instrument
Of man's first inventive genius typical (*produces a
    dagger*).

HORTENS.

O sir !

HAROLD.

          What! shudder and draw back from this?
Listen ! If all the men this little devil
And his brothers, long and short, have taken off
Were in one mighty heap piled up, they'd make
A pyramid of human skeletons
Piercing the skies.   Booming, noisy cannon
They have made ashamed, and the smaller guns
Hold but a lot in this great master's graveyard.
And look at its bright and glistening sides.—
Is it not wonderful how man can take
The black and shapeless metal from the earth
And make a thing of such exquisiteness?
How sharp its edges, that the keenest eye
Scarcely can see them; and that little point !
Is it not a wonderful instrument
Possessing a most wonderful record
For killing kings, betrayers, seducers,
And men in general ?—For, mark you well,
When this blade cuts through the heart or the lungs,
Or skull, or rips open the intestines

Of a man, not all the quackery invented
Can scarcely save him.   What, do you draw back
From such an honest, unassuming thing?

HORTENS.

I am a woman, sir, and until now
Am unaccustomed to such sights and words.
I pray you nothing you expect from me
Shall have in common anything with this.

HAROLD.

I did it but to try your honesty.
Begone before you add the crime of failure
To dishonesty and make a laughing stock
Of me.

HORTENS.

I swear that I am honest, sir,
Yet in my honesty but womanly.
I never thought of taking life, which has
A certain horror in it makes me shudder.

HAROLD.

No, woman, I would not have you, for the world,
Crimson your hands with human blood, much less
The sacred blood that courses in my veins.—
Partly therein to test you have I done this,
But ofttimes feigning force elicits truth.

HORTENS.

I see the import of your thought, and will
With all my better judgment act upon it (*takes the*
dagger).

12

HAROLD.

I like your looks ;—retire to yonder room,
And when you hear me strike upon this stand,
Enter and conduct you as you will.

HORTENS.

Sir, I would I might be more acquainted
How I am to act in this strange meeting.

HAROLD.

If you be honest, you will act aright;
Be guided by the moment's inspiration.

(Exit HORTENS.)

O time, from thy portentous womb
What monster may these moments hence
Not bring to birth ?   No good can come,
For either way lies infamy.
Quiet, my soul, my mother comes.

Enter CATHERINE, BOURNE, RICHARD, and HELEN.

CATHERINE.

Harold!

HAROLD.

No, madam, not another word;
"Twas for another that I sent for you.

BOURNE.

What want you with me that you bring me here?

HAROLD.

In good time I hope you may find out.
Behind yonder screen are places for you;
I pray you take them and abide events.

BOURNE.

As for myself, sir, you can see me here.

HAROLD.

Oh, be not presumptuous ; had I desired
Especially to see you, I had found you.

BOURNE.

Indeed you might ; I have not hid.

CATHERINE.

Maurice!

RICHARD.

Harold, something is very strange in this.

HELEN.

I know it can impart no good to us.

HAROLD.

Well, well, do as I bid you, or retire.

CATHERINE.

Have patience, Maurice; fear not my children.—
No sparrow falls except God will it so.
Harold, we will do your bidding, and trust
To Providence for our protection.

(*They go behind the screen*).

Enter HENCHMAN.

HAROLD.

Doctor, is my father disengaged?

HENCHMAN.

He is in consultation with his lawyer.

HAROLD (*aside*).

The fortune of the hour.—Remain here, sir.

(*Exit* HAROLD.

HENCHMAN.

There was meaning in that, *Remain here, sir*—
Remain?—Some villainy is stewing here.
How deadly calm his manner was!—Remain?
I think that should be spoken, *run away* (*going*).

Re-enter HAROLD, MALONE *and* GLASCO.

MALONE.

What want you, Harold, with us in such haste?

HAROLD.

In short—nay, Doctor, pray you do not go.

HENCHMAN.

My presence here—

HAROLD.

Nay, I would have you stay,—
In short, to hold some counsel with you all
Touching the matter of your impending suit.
Not that the subject is a pleasant one,
But since to meet and fight it we are compelled,
'Twere best we be prepared against the tricks
Of the opposing counsel.   What answers
Your wife to your petition for divorce?

MALONE.

O Harold, I would we might avoid it!

HAROLD.

Stuff, sir,—be man, not child: what says she?

GLASCO.

She denies her guilt and cross-complains against
    him
For divorce upon the ground of cruelty.

HAROLD.

The very boldness of a denial
Such as that covers one with amazement.
What hope has she to miss the proof
Of her repeated criminality?

MALONE.

Harold, I pray, do not refer to it;
It wrings my heart, and heaven knows how glad
Would I be here to end it all forever,
Did such a course not bring such infamy —
Such foul infamy—upon my children.

HAROLD.

Sir, if you have not more manhood in you
Than to talk of letting such dishonor
Pass unnoticed, condoned, forgiven,
I shall be justified in classing you
Among the apes, gratefully thanking God
My parentage is doubtful.   Full, complete,
  s the evidence of her adultery.

CATHERINE.

O God! no, no, no.

HAROLD.

What now; spies?---what's here?
(*He knocks the screen over.*)

By heavens, the very criminal themselves! (*strikes table*.)
Infamy, thou has reached thy highest tide
When such things be.

   Enter HORTENS.

    MALONE.

    Hortens! why are you here?

   HAROLD.

The uninvited guest that spoils our sport!
(*Aside*) Now let them work it out; it's not my play.

    HORTENS.

The disappointment is most agreeable;
I was afraid I had escaped your memory.

    HAROLD (*aside*).

The start is fair.

    CATHERINE.

    Amazement strikes me dumb.
Who are you, lady?   Maurice, who is she?

    BOURNE.

Till now I never saw her.

    HAROLD (*aside*).

     Very well.

    HORTENS.

Fear not, I am, none would harm you, madam,
But have come here to help you if you will.
Well, have you speech, sir? (*To* MALONE).

HENCHMAN (*to* MALONE).

Who is the woman ?

MALONE.

I know her not.

HAROLD.

Ha !

HENCHMAN.

I am a coward,
Else a moment since you called her Hortens.

HAROLD.

Well said, old fool ; I heard as much myself.

HORTENS.

So heard you all, and then he spake the truth,
But this last moment mysteriously
Has blotted me from out his memory.
'Tis possible, since he confessed to me
Your villainous attempt to ruin
Yonder woman, he has good reason
To forget me.

HAROLD (*aside*).

See, how she strikes him home !

HENCHMAN.

I see it all ; you have ruined your cause
By making a priest of your mistress.

HORTENS.

Go, you hireling !

HENCHMAN (*to* HORTENS).

      I have no case with you.
Confessed to her?   Oh, you old imbecile!—
I would rather be a dog than a fool.

      (*Exit* HENCHMAN.)

GLASCO.

To entice a lawyer in a scheme so vile!

      (*Exit* GLASCO.)

HAROLD.

Let them be gone,—the whole includes the parts.
What shall you say to this?

MALONE.

      That all she says
Is but a lie.

HORTENS.

      O you coward—liar!

CATHERINE.

Alas, that I have lived to see this day!

MALONE.

O Harold, to be rich is to be cursed
With such as these.   They are the vampires vile
That such the blackmail blood of all rich men,—
Believe her not.

HORTENS.

      Do you see this dagger?

CATHERINE.

Stop! Richard! Harold! Look to her, Maurice!

HORTENS.

No, do not touch me, for my cause is here.
Responsibility is overweighed in this.

CATHERINE.

O spare his life ; 'tis I am wronged, not you.

HORTENS.

Yes, you are wronged in me, and I in you,
And for our common wrongs I will kill you.

MALONE.

And this must be the payment for my love.

HAROLD.

Enough, enough, he has confessed enough !

HORTENS.

Madam, my work is done.

(*Exit* HORTENS, *hurriedly.*)

Enter CHARLOTTE.

HAROLD (*to* CATHERINE).

And you are pure!

CATHERINE.

Oh, miserable of women that I am,—
The day that proves me honest stabs me thus.

MALONE.

Charlotte, they are all against me.   Angel .
Of my life ! do not desert me, Charlotte.

HAROLD.

Is there no error here—no cunning scheme
To draw my weakness out ?   Where shall I look ?

On you (*to* CATHERINE), and blind my eyes with
    purity?
On you (*to* MALONE), and numb my soul with
    perfidy?
On me, and see the ghost of frailty,
The poor deceived and tortured cause of this?
O God, how useless seems my useless life!
Yet, if by any mighty act—some deed
Surpassing human strength or bravery,
Some action godlike in its virtue,
I could convince you of my overwhelming love,
And show that naught but honor has inspired
My every word and thought and act,—oh, then
This inward hell would burn with lesser heat.

CATHERINE.

I knew your honor, and for it honored you.

HAROLD (*to* MALONE).

Have you words,—what devil made you do this?

MALONE.

I am more sinned against than I have sinned.
We are not masters of our ways.

HAROLD.

                Well, well,
The reason savors of the vicious act,
And is as good as any you could give.
When you have learned the art to put the leaves
That, broken, mock the beauty of the rose,
Back in their cheerless sheathe and give them life,
You may reanimate this shattered state.
                  (*All stand apart.*)